WOLVES AND MEN

THE LUNAR MOTHER SERIES
BOOK 1

CHRISTOPHER SCHERRER

UNDER THE MOUNTAIN PUBLISHING

To Ratna and Taja
May the Lunar Mother always bless
and protect you

CONTENTS

1

He was shirtless and his small, but athletic frame was not spared the paint of the waning sun. The sun was always the most brilliant when it was about to dip under the horizon of the world. Especially here, where the tree-covered hills rolled into each other, creating a deep, rich valley in which a river flowed through and into the vast ocean. The red of the sky dipped and bled into the ocean turning it bright amber. The river became pure mercury as it slid through the land, eager to rejoin its place in the endless ocean, denying the boundaries of land.

He was wearing only jean shorts, no shirt, and no shoes. His deep blue-green eyes defied the power of the sun as he watched it get drawn into the water. Let the sun have his reign over the day. His mother would soon take her place in the cool vastness of her realm, night.

He closed his eyes and let the burned image on his retinas fade from the back of his eyelids. He opened his eyes to see that the ocean had won the battle, but the sun's light was still thrown out across the sky, portending his return tomorrow.

The reds of the sky were bleeding away into the water as the deep blue-black curtain of night continued to exert its dominance over the sky. As he looked out over the ocean, he felt the cool silver orb begin to rise over his hills. He almost forgot himself with the elation that leapt forward in his heart. He spun around and kneeled before her great beauty. Just as he had watched the old man sink into the ocean so too, with even more rapture and joy, he watched his majestic, Lunar Mother rise above his valley.

He watched as her generous, voluptuous shape rose, forming her perfect curvature. She grew fuller by the second; his eyes were wide and wanting. Her shape continued to fill out till it reached the zenith of her breast and then the curvature dissipated in no less beautiful a fashion.

The stars were beginning to come out of hiding from the old tyrant to be soothed by their mother, and they too looked at, and through him. They believed that they were the pride of the mother's flock. He stifled a smile. The mother blessed those whom she would, neither vanity nor pride played any part in that.

It always started this way.

The white hairs on the back of his neck stood on end and his muscles flexed involuntarily. He could feel his blood begin to warm and the wind was of no comfort. His skin began to turn red as his blood heated and tried to escape. His breath came out in ragged gasps as he tried to conquer the itch under his skin that would soon turn to pain. He felt a fire erupt in his belly and he arched his back as his neck and head shot forward. He barely kept from tipping over, balancing on his forearm. His eyes popped, threatening to fly from their sockets and his jaw tightened. His back arched like a cat and his leg shot out from underneath him as he fell on his side. His midsection, racked with convulsions, twisted and exploded outward, ripping his shorts clean in half. He barely noticed the loss as his now naked body thrashed on his rock.

His whole body roiled, and his blood was boiling, he could feel it. He gasped and shook as snot flew from his nose and saliva sputtered from his cracked mouth. Guttural inhuman sounds escaped him, and he knew that the forest animals were startled by the sudden disturbances. His legs kicked out and he thrashed on the ground. The rock scraped and dug into his body and that pain was a relief to what was happening to him just beneath the surface. His body hair was being forced out of their follicles as they grew longer. It began to thicken and cover the whole of his body in deep tan fur. His nose elongated and his jaw was removed from its proper place.

With his still human eyes, he was able to look up and see his mother. She was beautiful. He could almost see her smiling at him, but another convulsion shook his head down and around. He closed his eyes. He felt them being changed to be sharper, more focused than anything any human has ever known. His arms and legs broadened, and muscles erupted out from his skeletal structure. His ears grew up from his head, forming a sort of twin-peaked crown that marked him for everyone to know. His teeth grew and sharpened as his snout elongated to accommodate them. He felt his nails get pushed out of their places. They grew, hardened and sharpened, into curved blades. Sharp enough to rend flesh from underneath the thickest of hides and strong enough to support his weight on the steepest of climbs. He could feel his human tailbone elongate and shift upward, coating itself in the thick tan fur that now covered most of his body; his torso from the waist up was always left relatively bare.

He let out that which he could no longer stifle, a howl of pain that shook the birds from their places in the trees. His body gave one last convulsion, he breathed one last gasp, and all was still and silent.

The first thing he noticed was hunger, he was always hungry.

It burned and clenched his stomach muscles. He needed to eat. Through the darkness, he could smell them. Deer. He felt his saliva build up and drip from his open mouth. His eyes shot open, and he threw himself up from his rock. He looked upward and saw his beautiful mother. He bowed down low to her in gratitude and reverence, and he allowed his body to stretch to its full length as he let out a shrieking bloodthirsty howl of challenge.

The wolves of his valley never responded, and he expected no challengers. He was steward of this place, his home, given to him to be held in trust by both the old man and his mother. He let the howl die from his wet lips and he launched himself from his place on his rock. As he landed, he stretched out and began to tear through the wooded underbrush on his new frame using all four of his limbs. He could run upright, but why give up the exhilaration of using his full speed, whipping past trees and bushes, coming ever closer to his prey?

He pressed his body lower to the ground and forced himself to move faster. He could see everything as he ran through his forest. Even at the speed at which he now traveled he could pick out individual vein lines in the fern leaves as he rushed past, leaving nothing but wind and a faint smell that other prey knew to avoid. He knew he was leaving signs behind. No trace a normal person could detect, but it wasn't people that he had to worry about. His hands and feet were now the paws of the beast that his mother had blessed him with. The prints that were left in the soil could be traced by those living in his forest, but even that cognizant thought did nothing to slow the rush to his prey.

He could smell them, there were two of them.

As he lost himself in the smell his mind began to illustrate the picture and he could see them just as clearly as if he were watching them firsthand. One of them, the bigger of the two, a male, had been alerted by his howl and was pacing in and out of the river.

He could smell the creature's fear.

It was tangy and vibrant, almost like what a lemon would taste like but less sour, there was nothing like the smell of fear in his prey. As he ran through the woods, his eyes could still see the smallest detail of the forest around him, a trail of sap that slowly slid down the trunk of a nearby cedar. He saw an ant that was missing a leg as it trekked over the forest floor. But the smell of his prey created in his mind a second vision in which he watched his prey, inhaling even the smallest change in their scent. The deer was rotating his head back and forth looking up and down river. The deer didn't know it, but its head looked like a radar dish, constantly rotating. The deer's ears flicked forward and backward; he hadn't yet detected what hunted him. Soon it wouldn't matter.

He allowed himself to slow and maintain the downwind approach to his prey. He inhaled the scent again and knew that the smaller of the two, a female, was still drinking from the cool water. Should he kill them both? The thought made his mouth water as he let his animal side take over a little bit more. His thoughts began to diminish and become cloudy with pure instinct. His mind started to work. The only thing that mattered was the one thought of food and the kill.

He knew it was dangerous to let himself go like this especially since his lunar form's instinct was so powerful during the hunt. He might lose himself forever and remain a wild animal, to be hunted by those with the intellect to conquer his less sophisticated animal mind. His prey was more likely to outmaneuver him, and he was more likely to go hungry, which was also dangerous and could contribute to the erosion of who he was. But the power and apathy that came with those instincts was so great that he gave over to them willingly, just enough.

He slowed to a modest trot. He could begin to see the river as his mother shone down on it, reflecting her beauty for all to see. She was a master painter and under her glorious light, everything was touched with silver.

The doe raised her head from her drink and her head shimmered with the silver light of his mother.

He watched the pair in the moonlight for a few moments more, studying them, allowing his human mind to process the strengths of the prey, the angle of attack, the terrain, possible escape routes. The buck was bigger and would be more filling as a meal. He was farther away but already alert, unsteady, and jumpy. As soon as William moved to attack, the buck would bolt, the female would be a half step behind. They would probably run down river till they could cross and run up the opposing slope. The female was calmer. It was odd that the male hadn't relaxed yet. It had been some time since his howl and there was no way that the deer could have sensed his approach. It was troubling to his human mind that the animals of his forest were less docile than they used to be. As if his fair rule over the woods made the creatures uncomfortable in some way.

Just like the people he used to live among.

He shook that thought away as soon as it surfaced. This was not the time. The doe would make a much better target. She was still drinking from the river and soon they would leave, her smell had changed to something resembling contentment which meant she had quenched her thirst. She raised her head one final time and turned away from him. That was all the opening he needed. He sprang forward and the male, as predicted, bolted a touch faster than the doe. The doe's butt lowered as she kicked off the shallow bedrock of the river. She kicked up a great spray of water like a curtain, a curtain that he parted with his great shape as he leapt and came down, forepaws first, on the hindquarters of the female.

The doe screamed and fell into the water with a splash. He used his great upper body strength to heave himself over the body of the fallen deer as she kicked and screamed, trying to get up. He brought himself to her neck and snapped down on her jugular vein. He felt the warm gush of her lifeblood spew out from around his massive jaws. The deer continued to scream and kick but the kicks were quickly becoming less forceful, less panicked and her screams were less loud. He continued to apply the pressure, squeezing her neck with his teeth. The deer could only gasp for breath now, which was becoming more ragged and shallow.

He buried his nose deep in her neck. No animal smelled like this, except right before death. It was so much more intimate than the smell of any other emotion, even fear. It was the smell of submission to the inevitable. He could feel her very weak, rapid pulse slow and soon there was nothing. He held her in his mouth for another moment then let her go.

She was wide-eyed and her tongue was hanging out of

her small gaping mouth, leaving a trail of her rich blood into the water. He retracted his claws from her flank and dipped his blood-stained jaws into the river. He scrubbed his snout with his paws and cleaned his claws. He kicked himself upright and, with water dripping from his face and arms, he looked toward his mother, and he howled his victory to her. His royal howl rang out from the sides of his valley as each tree echoed and sang his call back to each other. He looked at his mother in her rightful place in the sky and bowed low in gratitude to her, thanking her for her generosity.

He gripped the carcass in his claws, and he threw the great weight of her over his shoulder and walked back to the riverbank. He began to trudge up the hill. He had passed a large rock on the way down to the river. It would make a perfect dinner table. Just because he looked like an animal didn't mean he had to necessarily eat like one. He could eat his kill on the relatively clean surface of a rock instead of the dirt floor of his forest. Royalty had to abide by some rules of etiquette.

He walked for a time, knowing that the carcass he carried was leaking all over the place. It didn't matter. The trail would go unnoticed and untraced. There was nothing to challenge him here, not as he was now. He came to the large boulder he had passed and walking up the hill past it a ways, he turned and jerked the dead animal down upon the stone's surface.

He sat down on his haunches. He straightened his back, just slightly, and with both his claws he lifted the great bulk of the animal and ripped her hind leg off. He always got a small amount of satisfaction out of that small gesture, a small reminder of the power he now wielded and what he had not possessed only a short while ago. He lifted the leg and sucked the blood from the flesh and the marrow from the bone. Still warm. He let the nourishment sink into his empty stomach and he closed his eyes. Calm and contentment flooded his body and mind. Nowhere in all of the human idea of civilization was there a feeling like this. The feeling of truly earning your nourishment and the contentment and sense of natural order that accompanied that feeling; this was the true meaning of life. Death was necessary and through death, life is given to others, the natural order. He opened his eyes and tore into his kill with a fervor that few humans could imitate.

He could taste the meat in ways that he never could as a human. The deer meat he ate was tender as if it had marinated in its own blood. The pulpy flesh was filling, and he savored every bite. He consumed the first leg in minutes while still enjoying every flavor of it. He ripped off the second leg and devoured it as well.

As he continued to eat, he felt his stomach begin to fill. He noticed just how much he could eat now; the downside however was that he had to eat this much every time he was blessed by his mother. His mother. He looked up and could see her pale visage through the tree branches. She was in her Heaven, and all was as it should be. He smiled to himself and continued to eat his kill.

The smell and the trail of blood he had left behind had begun to attract others from his forest. The other predators of his forest, the coyotes, and of course his cousins the wolves. He watched them approach him as he continued to tear into the side of the carcass in front of him. They were majestic animals in grey and white and black fur. They walked and hunted with his permission, and they bowed to his supremacy. The old grey of the pack was standing inside the shade of a nearby tree. His golden eyes were looking at the fresh kill on the rock.

He remembered the first time the two of them had met. It was a night like this, a little over a year ago.

He had been reborn for the first time and for the first time he had had to deal with his animal instincts as well as cope with what had happened to him on his human side. The two sides were a jumble of shock and raw emotions. His human side panicked seeing his hands had turned to claws and he couldn't speak, only utter guttural dog-like growls. He was hungry and his animal side sought the hunt. He could barely keep the two sides separate and he almost lost himself in his blood lust. His nose had picked up prey and it was all he could do to not run off after them with the sole purpose of killing.

As he wrestled with these two sides of himself, he turned around and there was the biggest grey wolf he had ever seen. He was standing on a rock outcropping above him on the hill. The wolf bared his teeth and issued the challenge his gold eyes locked upon his target.

He didn't know what to do, he had enough to deal with and then it happened. His animal side took over and pure instinct flooded his conscience. He met the challenge with a howl, and he jumped up the ledge and attacked.

The old grey was not the alpha of the pack for nothing. He jumped down and to the side easily dodging the newcomer's clumsy uphill attack. Before he could land and pivot back toward the wolf, the old grey jumped up and snapped at his tendons catching his leg just below the knee. He howled with the surprise of the attack though for some reason the razor-sharp teeth of the wolf did little real damage. He twisted around and brought both of his hands down in a hammer blow upon the wolf's snout.

This attack was not anticipated, and the old grey was thrown off his leg. The wolf's snout was bleeding from the blow, but he wasn't finished. The old grey was the alpha of the pack, and no intruder was going to usurp him. The wolf growled and jumped up. Its attack was blocked by his raised arm and the old grey was left dangling, almost comically, from his arm refusing to let go.

His animal instinct was to kill this challenger, but his mental fog lifted, and he saw the creature for what it was, a proud predator protecting his pack and territory. He felt a deep understanding with the wolf as it hung from his arm. The wolf's gold eyes were still hostile, but he meant no harm to the creature. However, he could afford no rivals in his forest. He lifted his arm and the weight of the wolf over his head and punched it in its underside with his other hand. He swung the beast down on the dirt and grabbed its snout in his hand. He removed the jaws from his forearm and clamped the wolf's teeth shut. The wolf worked to free itself twisting its body left and right.

He yanked the wolf down to the ground forcing a yelp from the poor beast and looked it in the eye. The wolf stopped struggling and he let go of the proud beast. The wolf raised itself up and with his pride and dignity on display, turned away from him. He walked back to the rest of the pack with his tail hanging low. His human side almost felt sorrow for his proud opponent, but this too was the natural order. There could be only one alpha and there was no room for competitors. He did what felt right and a howl of triumph erupted from his lungs.

He was joined by the rest of the pack and their song echoed long and loudly through his valley. Every wolf of the pack gave their support except the old grey. He looked down at the animal and the grey stood there. He let his gaze harden and the old grey did what it had never had to do in its life, it bowed its head and put its snout into the dirt, acknowledging its new alpha.

Now, back in the present, the old grey waited a respectful distance away, waiting to see if the alpha would share any of the kill. He smiled at his family and turned his attention to the coyotes. He bared his teeth and issued a challenge to them. They retreated to the safety of the trees, and he shoved the rest of the unfinished carcass to his pack. As the wolves finished what remained of the deer, he turned toward the intruders and raising himself to his full height growled again. The coyotes looked up at the wolves' alpha with wide, fear-stricken eyes, and without a sound, they disappeared back into the woods.

He turned to his pack and jumped down from his rock. The old grey had his snout deep inside the skeleton of the deer, but it knew when he was close. The old grey pulled its head out from the skeleton and lowered its head to the ground in respect.

William trotted back into the trees. He knew that the wolves looked at him as their alpha and he was always troubled by that thought. Had the wolves of his valley come to depend on him? He was still human most of the time, after all. What if one day he had to leave? He wasn't planning on leaving, ever. But old human habits die hard, and he couldn't shake the feeling that things were not always going to be as they are now.

He pushed the thought away and dropped down onto all fours as his pack once again approached him. He glanced behind him and saw the wolves nuzzle the ground and look around their surroundings. This was the best part of the night, and he leapt forward. The wolves were only a split second behind him as he raced downhill with his pack. This was true happiness.

He tore over the ground running fast. He dodged trees as he half ran, half leapt down the hillside. The rest of his pack moved with him and flowed through the trees like a wave of seawater. He made a sharp, sudden turn to the left and the rest of the pack flowed behind him like a great mass moving over the land. He slowed his pace and snipped at the hindquarters of a young male running beside him. The black male kicked out and away from the bite and snapped back at him. He was quicker and kicked out to meet the nose of the young black. It stumbled for a moment but regained its balance, slowing to let him pass, the black conceding to the defeat. He glanced back at the black and watched as a smaller female raced up from behind the embarrassed male and she bit him in the tail. It yelped and spun around facing its tormentor, but the female, who was also a beautiful black with a white starburst on her chest, leapt up and over the male and landed lower on the slope losing none of her speed in the maneuver.

He would have laughed but in his current form, it came out as a short bark. The female replied with a bark of her own and soon the whole pack was barking, snipping, and playing with each other. He looked over and saw two males tackle a bigger male as they all collapsed in a heap of legs and teeth. They all got up and were soon amid the pack once again. He led his family over the river. And with a leap that none of his pack could match he cleared the river easily, landing softly on the opposite riverbank. Some of the younger males attempted the jump and just ended up splashing into the middle of the river. The rest veered off and charged through a nearby shallow ford in the river. He waited for a large amount of the wolves to cross before he turned and led his pack up the opposite slope. The pack raced and darted through the trees chasing each other up the slope of the valley.

He saw the old grey chasing two younger females off to his left. He didn't mind the old man getting some exercise. He was old but still one of the strongest in the pack and he would make a fine mate since his mate had died sometime before he had been reborn. He could never quite understand what had happened, either that or his pack was being vague on purpose but what happened to the old grey's mate had not been communicated to him, and he hadn't sought the answer.

Wolf communication was very detailed, though not in words. Wolf language was a complex series of vocals, scents, and movements, their fur coloring was a huge part of that and even the smallest flick of an eye muscle was an important bit of information to other wolves. His human mind got in the way sometimes and he found it difficult to understand some of the more complex things his pack would try to communicate to him. This was one topic that the pack was uncomfortable sharing, and he wasn't ready to make the endeavor more painful by making them explain it in a way that he could understand, so he was content to let whatever happened to the old grey's mate remain in the past.

He led his pack up the hill. Much of the night had passed already and as they approached the summit of the valley wall, he looked up in the night sky. His mother was already well on her descent from her throne in the night sky, so he quickened the pace.

The pack raced him almost straight up the hillside. They burst through the tree line and skidded to a halt. He stood with his forest and his pack behind him, and he took two steps forward. He sensed them following him still and he turned. His family was stepping forward to follow him. He bared his teeth and growled low in his throat. The wolves stopped mid-step and turned back toward the tree line. He nodded his head and turned back toward the summit of the hill. He walked the last hundred feet and stood at the very top of his valley. He raised himself upright on the soft dirt that covered the stone of the hillside and with his back to his Lunar Mother he faced his pack, his valley, his home.

As he looked out over his family, he raised his head and once again howled in triumph to the night sky. His pack joined him in his celebration and the sound of wolves was the only sound anything in the valley could hear. Birds took flight and deer fled from their places. Rabbits and squirrels ran for their various burrows and the coyotes huddled close together.

This valley was his and his pack's. Wolves ruled here, now and forever.

He lowered himself on all fours and looked over his pack. They all watched him. The night was almost over, and he couldn't let his pack see him change back into his frail human form. He looked at each one of his pack mates in turn, and his eyes fell on two adolescent males. They were both grey with black stripes, their golden eyes shone in the reflected moonlight, brothers. He looked at them as they panted still trying to recover from the long run.

He hadn't seen these two cubs before and he was stricken with how frail they looked, how much they still depended on their mother who stood just behind them. When will the son become the father and his circle close? He wasn't sure and he wondered if he would ever have children of his own. Not with these animals, proud and noble though they were. But there was nothing for him in the human world either. He was a freak not meant to undertake the ritual of parentage. Besides, how could he pass on this gift that, with the wrong person, would almost certainly cause unlimited suffering for those around him? And that would be just one more thing that he would have to live with. One more mistake, one more misjudgment that had caused so much pain even in his somewhat short life.

He pried his interested eyes away from the two pups and continued to survey his pack. These wolves were strong, and they had never had any history of upheaval. In fact, in the history of the pack told by the old ones, his coming to this valley was the first event of some significance to happen for eons. As his eyes slid off the last wolf in the group, he readied his last command of the night. He had made the command every time he changed but seeing them go never got any easier. His wolves always seemed so dejected, and their tails would hang low. Even though he tried to brace himself for the unfair guilt trip dumped on him time and again by his pack, time and again he died just a little on the inside. He knew what the pack expected of him and the worst knot of guilt he suffered from these days was that he couldn't run, hunt, or lead his pack all the time. His kingship was measured in single nights, not consecutive days. Some-times he had such horrible thoughts like some massive predator would break into the valley and he would not be around to protect his pack, though his pack would wait for him, and they would line up for the slaughter, scanning the hillside for their alpha that would never come.

But those were nightmares and horrible daydreams. He breathed a deep breath and barked out twice. At the sound of his command, all the wolves looked up at him with wide, shocked eyes. He didn't allow his eyes to drop away from the betrayed looks he now received, and he repeated his two barks.

Minutes rolled by as the Lunar Mother continued her unstoppable descent below the horizon, and just like every other night, he was forced to stare down his pack and by sheer force of will, force them to disperse through the valley.

One by one the wolves turned from their places on the hilltop and began their long slow march back to their den. He watched as each wolf of his pack stared at him as if to ask, "Why are you sending us away? What did we do wrong?" A question asked but could never be answered, a question that broke his heart not to be able to answer. He wanted them to understand who and what he was, but his fear of them not understanding and attacking him while he was human was more than enough of a fear-driven incentive to remain silent to the accusatory, cold stares of his pack.

When the last wolf had turned away and disappeared into the tree line, he stood up on his hind legs, dropped his head, and breathed heavy, ragged breaths. Sometimes withstanding those cold stares, where once they were warm and welcoming, was almost too much for him to bear.

He lowered himself on all fours and took off at full speed away from the retreating members of his pack. He rushed along the ridgeline. He glanced beside him, and the Lunar Mother was already touching the horizon and sinking lower by the second. He pushed himself to run faster. Not only was he racing against the moonset, but he was also racing against being followed by his pack. He had taken too long on this night and now he was paying for it.

At a unique pairing of two white pine trees, he turned and dove down the slope of his valley. The sky was already well-lit with the dawn, and he had no trouble seeing possible obstacles. He pushed himself to reckless speeds as he crashed down the slope. He had to get to his burrow beneath the redwood before the moon set.

It was there that he lived. For some reason after he changed, and his wolf form was taken away from him, he was always drained and extremely vulnerable. It took him a day or more sometimes to fully recover and for that time he was weak as a newborn and twice as helpless. No one lived in his valley to protect him from harm. While he was a wolf, he was the king of the valley, but as a human, he was just as susceptible to attack and being killed as any creature.

He crashed through the ground shrubs, thundering over and through the dead pine needles that were on the forest floor. He should be there by now, where was it? And then he spotted the old redwood. In his haste, he had veered off target, but he quickly turned and kicked off the ground toward his haven. He raced around the base of the tree to the hidden portal and just as he felt the Lunar Mother wane, he tumbled through the passage in the depression that made up his home. He was able to turn just in time to hide the portal from being seen and with that, the last of his mother's sway vacated. He fell backward, blacking out before he hit the soft dirt floor.

2

He awoke groggy and sore.
What time is it?
What day is it?

His abdomen screamed as he tried to prop himself up. He decided to lay back down flat on his back. The floor of his shelter was soft and warm and after all, it's not like he had to go to work. He smiled at the thought, he may not have work, but survival was a daily task. There wasn't a Walmart down the street, and he didn't have a refrigerator either. What he caught or hunted today is what he ate today.

Looking at the ceiling of his shelter he thought about just how much time he had spent in his forest. The heavy smell of earth filled his nose. The forest that could kill him on any given day had been kind to him and through some trial and error he had learned to live with it and this place seemed to have accepted him. The ceiling of his burrow arched over his head and was made with various logs that made a checkerboard pattern. They supported a thick layer of mud and clay that was meshed with other smaller branches and pine needles.

This little burrow had taken a long time to build. His mind reached back to those early days. He was so new to this world, but he had a small idea of what had to be done. Oddly enough, he had found this giant redwood on the first day. It had a sad feeling surrounding it. The great tree had a chunk taken out of it by some fire or another. The scar remained, though it had begun to heal itself. It would be many years, if ever, before the wound was fully healed. But the indention of the tree lent itself to be a perfect shelter and he had begun digging out his burrow floor, which he now rested upon. He had dug, and cleared out, maybe two feet or more of the forest floor that covered a ten-foot area at the base of the scarred redwood.

He glanced around at his burrow and smiled. It was a good home, as good a one as one could ever need, and he had built it himself. Those first days had been filled with fears that some animal would come and tear his burrow down, or claim it for their own.

He was not as unprepared as some guy who just got up and walked into a forest one day. He had brought with him tools and some supplies. To get the ceiling beams, he went out with his woodsman axe and through a few days' work, he had gathered several logs and smaller branches to make the frame of his shelter. It was maybe the easiest part of the whole project. To get the shelter to be waterproof, and also to mask his scent as well as the smell of food and other things that would attract the unwanted attention of the forest animals, he knew he would have to seal his roof. This was a lot easier said than done. When one did not have mortar or cement, he had to make do with what was at hand, and what was at hand was mud and clay from the nearby riverbed. The only problem was that his chosen burrow was a good mile or two from it.

He remembered taking handfuls of mud and clay from the river and climbing the hillside before dumping the clay on the roof frame and going back down for more. It didn't occur to him until the second day that he could heap the mud and clay on some tree branches and carry a lot more up the hillside per trip than with just his bare hands. Even with the new technique it had still taken him the better part of three days to finish his roof.

He inhaled the familiar scents of his home and his forest. The air mixed with the cedar of the nearby pines. And under it all, the rich musky scent of the earth of the forest floor.

This place had sustained him for what? A year? Two? He really didn't know and right now, did it matter?

Despite the protests of his abdomen, he raised himself up off his floor. He had to bend over to avoid touching his ceiling but that was ok. He didn't spend much time here; he always had so much work to do. He looked behind him at his bed. It was a collection of logs and branches interlaced with pine needles. Deer skins covering the whole thing with a great bear skin blanket to keep him warm on those cold wintery nights. It was the most comfortable bed he had ever slept on and the last he felt he would ever need.

Next to his bed was a little dresser that he had also built himself. It wasn't so much a dresser as a three-sided wooden frame where he kept what remained of his 'normal world' possessions, the least of which were his normal clothes. He frowned as he noticed that he only had one full set of normal clothes left. It didn't really matter though he spent the majority of his time in his deer and bear skins. Through them, he had been able to keep warm last winter and been able to function out here away from any other human being.

This was life, not just some facsimile of a perceived existence that had to be filled with the latest technology or gadgets. Life. Most people would say that he was running away from life to hide out in the woods like some estranged hermit. What did other people know? Had they survived out in the wilderness for any period of time?

Through survival he had found that many of his 'civilized' accoutrements could be shed, even names were expendable. His real name had meant very little to him out here. William Hadrian Setford. What did that name mean anymore? What use was that name to him out here? To say nothing about an even more useless set of numbers, like his social security number. The United States Government couldn't or wouldn't touch him out here. Why would they? He had been gone over a winter and more than a year over that. He hadn't been paid any money nor had he paid taxes. It probably didn't occur to them that there was a young man out there who simply refused to live like everybody else.

He smiled and snorted out a laugh, *a crazy person would, that's who.*

Was it really crazy to live with yourself, test yourself against nature, and to have found true happiness? Maybe, as far as he knew he was a singularity in the human condition. Why give up all the comforts of modern living to go live among the mosquitoes and wolves of the forest?

The wolves. His pack was his family now, even though he only got to run with them one night out of the month. He looked forward to his nights with his pack.

A loud rumbling and squeezing of his abdomen brought him back to reality. He had to eat. He was hungry, but it was a different type of hunger, more a nagging urge than a desire that drove him.

He leaned down, grabbed his rich brown deerskin pants, and pulled them on. They had gotten a little loose since the last time he had worn them. He grabbed his black bear skin vest and raccoon skin hat and finished dressing himself. He was glad that he didn't have a mirror. He probably looked like an idiot, but his clothes were functional and out here he was the biggest trendsetter since Calvin Klein. He grabbed his coyote skin bag and his fishing pole and pried open his burrow door.

The sunlight that slanted through the trees was a warm yellow that showed the dew and microscopic debris and dust that was ever present in the woods. It was morning and the sun was just lending his warmth to the forest floor. He could see his breath as he stepped outside. He inhaled the scents of this place, fresh air, and sweet smell of the ceder, underlined with the rick must of the earth all around him, were so familiar to him but no less appreciated. He looked up and smiled at his redwood. The solid old man had plenty of good years left in him and he was thankful for the companionship. Was it crazy to consider a tree a friend? Who cares what other people think? Let them spend a few years out here and see what orthodox conceptions they cling to.

He set his fishing pole and bag down and resealed his burrow's portal. The clay and mud of his ceiling did an amazing job of covering his smell from the surrounding areas and he was glad of it. Human noses were so weak compared to other animals. Good thing he could tap into some animal skills of his own.

He stood up, grabbed his bag and pole, and made his way down to the river. He was always cautious of his woods, no matter what kind of day it was. By now he was sure that he had lost any trace of his 'civilized human' smell, but that did not guarantee his safety. If living out here had taught him anything it was that life was never safe and to stay alive you must be cautious, pick your battles, and sometimes, kill. Life was a constant struggle out here and he had found that he was well-suited for it. As well as any human could be and sometimes better than any human could imagine.

His thoughts kept returning to his nights spent as an animal. This was normal for him. He was always a little sad after he awoke from his nocturnal activities shared with his pack. It wasn't easy to let go of that power and those smells. Seeing the forest through animalistic eyes was something he wished he could do all the time, not just once a month. But being in Heaven one night a month would have to be enough.

Sighing, he continued walking toward his river. He was constantly scanning his surroundings. He looked past the rich brown trees to his left as he walked upon the dead pine needles that made up the carpet of the forest floor. He hadn't mastered walking silently yet. He had read in stories such as *The Last of the Mohicans* that Native Americans were able to walk without a sound through their forests in their leather moccasins. He didn't need moccasins, or rather chose to go without, the calluses on his feet were thick enough to protect him from all but the sharpest of stones underfoot, but being able to walk without a sound to his weak human ears would go a long way to give him some confidence about stealth and avoiding being heard by the predators of this place.

He made slow steady progress down the hillside. He knew that his death could strike at any moment, and it wouldn't be because of his shoes or his worldly possessions. His death would be at the hands of a hungry predator. That was the law out here. The natural order of things and if you wanted to live another day you had to play by nature's rules.

He stopped just in sight of the river and scanned to his

left and then to his right. He couldn't hear anything, and he didn't see anything. When he was sure the area was vacant, he moved slowly out onto the riverbank. He kept looking and listening for anything. His wolf pack could be anywhere and as he was right now; he was not their alpha, but prey to be hunted. There were bears out here too, as well as coyotes. Come to think about it, a lot of animals shared his home, predators that really wouldn't think twice about ending him.

He set his bag down and prepared his fishing pole. Yes, he was fragile compared to the other animals, but hadn't his survival proven he was made of at least equal stuff as wolves? He opened his bag to pull out the small box which contained his fishing tackle. This bag had been one of the first things he had made out here.

He had planned to come out here and live. It was not just some crazy idea he had hatched and gone off half-cocked. He had planned and prepared for several months. His preparation had included taking several frontiersman classes on how to survive in the wild. He had learned how to skin an animal, how to make traps, and how to gather food from the forest. He had also invested in some sewing classes.

He had bought a fifty-pound weight compound bow to hunt with. And he had learned to use it before he had left the 'real' world. Why not just bring a rifle? The philosophical answer, for him, was that animals didn't have any real defense against firearms. The practical answer was that it was possible to make more ammunition for his bow, whereas with a gun he would have to buy more bullets, and where was there a trading post out here, or money for that matter?

The skin that made up his bag was from the first animal he had killed while in his new home.

He had only been in his valley a few days. He always

carried his knife with him no matter what he was doing. In those first days, while he was building his burrow, he was aware of how exposed he was to this new world. He was carrying a load of mud up the hillside. He had been a little tired, and who wouldn't be? Walking a mile or two uphill per trip with an armful of mud and clay would be enough to wear out anybody.

It was the late afternoon when he heard it, a desperate feeling shattered his fragile sense of security and safety. He looked around and he couldn't see anything but somehow, he knew that a predator was nearby, and he was the target. He panicked and started to run. He tore through the woods to get to his burrow. The underbrush clung and ripped at his denim jeans, but he was only aware of how far away from the safety of his burrow he was. Not that an open frame over a shallow hole in the ground was any kind of protection. And with that thought, he stopped running and pressed his back against a nearby tree. He had become very calm as he dropped his load of mud and clay, and he unsheathed his knife.

This was the reason he had wanted to live out here among nature, to test himself and live by a higher code of life. Life had to be earned out here and there was no 'safe house' to run to.

He pulled the moderately sized blade up to his chest and held it at the ready. It was a big knife, not quite a machete but bigger than a Bowie knife. He heard the creature only seconds before the animal burst through the underbrush. It was tan in color with black eyes and a black nose. That was all his mind could take in before the creature jumped up and attacked. His mind registered the snarling of the beast in midair and it was pure reactive instincts that brought his knife to pierce the underside of his attacker. He looked at the animal as it hung for a few perfect seconds in midair. He looked down into the animal's eyes and he could see that there was no hatred there, only what had to be. This was a hunter who had hunted something that could fight back. In that second, through this animal's eyes, he understood the price for carelessness and this predator had paid nature's tax for its negligence.

The weight of the thing pushed it farther down on his knife and his arm was simply unable to hold the weight of the animal. As his arm dropped the predator slid from his knife and collapsed down on the ground, a pool of blood gathering beneath its already dead corpse.

He had taken enough classes to know that the blood would attract some unwanted attention, so he had dragged the dead coyote off away from his burrow. He stashed the carcass under some bushes and ran back to his burrow to get some of his rope. He came back to the carcass and began to skin, and butcher it.

He had let the blood soak into the forest floor, while the strips of meat he had carved off were laid out on some plastic from a tarp, which he had brought with him for this purpose. He knew that, while the coyote didn't give a lot of meat for an animal it would probably be too much for him to eat safely in one sitting. After he had cleaned and gutted the thing, he wrapped up the meat and bones from the dead coyote and carried them away from the butcher site and his home.

He had built a fire and cooked what meat he was going to eat, turned out that it was only about a quarter of the animal. The rest he smoked and dried so it would keep. When he was done the sun had already set and he needed to get back to his home. He made one last trip down to the river to clean the bones and the skin.

To wash the smell and the blood away he used a bag net. He rinsed off every piece of the skeleton and scrubbed the skin. He placed everything into the bag net and tied it to a nearby tree with the bag in a nice little alcove in the river stream that had some good water movement. The natural motion of the river would continue to rinse the smell off the articles and clean the skin.

The next day, he retrieved his bag. The skeleton pieces were white and cold, he could detect no smell of blood on them, enough to make him secure in the fact that no other animals would be able to smell it either. He left the skeleton pieces in the bag, and he retrieved the skin. It was a sizable pelt, and he knew that it would make a great bag to keep his stuff all in one place. He might need to pick up quickly if something ever happened, a fire, or a bear crashing through his home one day. You could never be too prepared out here.

It had taken a few days to cure the pelt. He stretched and hung the pelt out between two trees, allowing it to air dry, he de-haired it, applied a brain oil solution, softened it, and smoked it. When it had completely dried, he finished the majority of the sewing that was necessary for his bag. He had sewn a leather strip onto the skin to use as a shoulder strap.

That bag had been with him since the very beginning and now, as he reached inside to grab his small tackle box, he was really glad that he had made the thing. He set the tackle box down next to him. He placed his fishing pole across his legs and pulled out a little of his fishing line. He then opened his tackle box and grabbed a bone fishhook that he had made. With the excess fishing line, he fastened the hook to his pole.

He stood up and looked around him listening to his forest. He always had to remember where he was and he was always careful not to lose himself in what he was doing for too long. Satisfied that he was still alone, or as alone as could be expected, he started rooting around in the mud and dirt next to the river. He could usually find worms near the riverbank and today was no exception. With a practiced hand, he slipped a caught worm onto his hook and cast his line out into the river.

As the hook slipped beneath the cold, rushing water of his river, he indulged in closing his eyes and letting the sunbathe his face and body. He could feel the warmth building around him and he was happy to let the sun's rays warm him. He inhaled and let the aroma of the forest be absorbed through him.

He held his pole in his hands allowing it to be tugged by the moderate current of the river. The water bubbled and washed over the rocks and stones of its bed making the water dip and turn white in some places. There was always good fishing to be had here. Still some days he had walked away with nothing. He hoped today would not be one of those days.

He waited and guided his hook and line on a slow serpentine pattern through the various currents before placing his pole into a premade pile of rocks and clay that he used as a pole catcher.

He scanned his surroundings and the treetops. The river was just as blue as it had been a moment ago. The sun was painting the trees a vibrant green and added a warm golden hue to the air around him. The smell of cedar pine and clean water wafted around him. He slapped at his neck with honed reflexes and pulled away a red-splattered mosquito. He felt a slight unease; he began to feel very exposed out here next to the river.

He unsheathed his knife as he continued to look around

himself. He inhaled, but couldn't smell anything, which was nothing new. He glanced up the hillside at the majestic trees as they kept their constant vigil over the river. A wind gently blew through the valley, and he could feel the sun's warmth being stolen on its gentle breath. He looked across the riverbank then turned to look behind him.

Nothing.

His instincts had served him well since he had begun living out here and he was not likely to dismiss this feeling of unease.

Something was watching him.

This was not uncommon. He often felt the forest's eyes upon him, but there was an underlying threat to the feeling now. The image of a rat in a maze came to mind. Something was not right, and he would not allow himself to relax.

He continued to survey his surroundings. An attack or something of equal danger was coming, he could feel it. The hairs stood up on the back of his neck and it wasn't because of the wind. He turned his body toward the river and scanned the trees and underbrush.

He saw her, a black wolf with a white starburst patch on her chest.

He recognized the female from his last night with his pack. She was beautiful and she was looking right at him. He couldn't see any hatred or malice in her stare, just a contemplative look, studying this new entity curiously. How long had she been there? He didn't know but he didn't sheath his weapon either. The two stood staring at each other from across the river. If the river had not separated them, she could have attacked at any time, but she seemed content to just watch.

He stood there poised and at the ready. The familiar weight of his knife put a comfortable strain upon his strong right hand. The river continued to run, and the wind continued to blow moving the tree branches and the underbrush around them. The two held each other in their gaze, neither bowing to the other. A sudden shift to his right caught his peripheral vision and he shifted his attention to his pole which was being pulled and moved against its stone cradle.

He grabbed the pole with his free hand, throwing his knife down to pierce the ground with the blade ready to be withdrawn. He positioned the pole in his hands and with practiced movements he spun the line, tugged, released, and drew in more line. The fish on the other end was strong and felt to be sizable. He worked his pole and concentrated on the fish. He kept some of his attention on the she-wolf across the river who still had not moved. She continued to watch him. A year ago, that might have really freaked him out. As it was, he was content to share the spectacle with her.

He reeled in more line and tugged. He let a small amount of line run out again and with a practiced jerk and pull, he heaved his catch up onto the riverbank. The fish was about a foot long and it started jumping and writhing around on the ground, his bone hook fastened through the fish's cheek. He laid his pole down pulling out some slack through the line.

He knelt next to the fish and glanced across the river toward the she-wolf. She was gone. He scanned the surrounding landscape, but the black she-wolf was nowhere to be seen. He didn't feel uneasy about the sudden disappearance. Was it disappointment? The slap of a fin upon the ground brought him back to his task at hand.

He hunched down next to the struggling fish and with both hands grabbed its dorsal fin. The fish shook and wiggled in his strong grip, waving back and forth in the air. He brought the animal down with a swipe upon a rock, cracking the skull of the animal. It stopped struggling. He held the dead animal up and tested its weight in his hands. This would be enough for today.

Gripping the fish in one hand he removed his hook. He picked up his pole and knife and made his way back to his bag and tackle box. He laid his pole down on the ground and sheathed his knife. Pulling out the net from his bag he placed the fish in the net and propped it up against a tree. He undid the bone hook from his fishing line and placed it back in his box. He picked up his pole and rewound his line. He placed his pole across his bag strap so he could grab both with one hand and stepped over to his net.

He picked up the net and walked to the very edge of the river. He let the icy water flow over his feet and toes, and he dunked his net into the water. He let the river water run over and around his fish and when he was satisfied that it was clean, he retrieved the net.

Holding the net in one hand he picked up his bag and pole with his other hand and began his trek up the hillside. The appearance of the she-wolf made him move a bit more cautiously than he had earlier this morning and his progress was slow and calculated. He made his way up the hillside to a small clearing, which he had claimed long ago as his kitchen area. It was far enough away from his burrow that he didn't worry about animals tracking him in between the two places. He dropped his bag and pole in the middle of the clearing next to his fire pit. He walked back and strung up his net on a rope that he had hung upon a sizable tree branch long ago for this purpose. He set to work gathering wood for his breakfast fire.

He set a sizable pile of gathered wood next to his bag and pole and his dug-out fire pit.

He sat down upon a wide slice of wood that he had cut away from a fallen tree and moved here so he would have a place to sit. No matter how often he had tried to balance the thing, it remained just a little wobbly. He reached into his bag and pulled out a simple grey, waterproof box that was the size of his small tackle box. He considered this box to be his most prized possession. He opened the box and pulled out his flint stone and Swiss army knife and placed it in his lap. Leaning over the pit he placed prepared tinder and wood shavings from the box. He closed the box and set it beside him as he dragged some wood from his pile over to the little mound of tinder and shavings.

He had his kindling and small branches set aside to be added once the flame had caught. Taking his knife he set it to his flint stone. Scraping the stone with the edge of the knife he sighed as a copious amount of sparks flew onto the small pile of tinder. Even in the bright morning sunlight the sparks still left burn impressions on his retinas. He saw a fine trail of smoke go up and he knelt close to blow on the pile.

The smoke increased and soon an infant flame leapt up licking and consuming the pile of tinder. He placed some kindling on the flame. The flames grew and licked at the dry morsels of fuel. He added more kindling, some twigs, and branches till the fire had grown to its adolescent stages. He let the fire warm him as he watched the flames dance and sway with the light wind. He had learned some time ago that the best way to fight fear and loneliness in the wild was to build a fire. If you want to change the channel just add another log. Fire was truly an amazing thing, no wonder cavemen and the ancient Greeks thought of this as the stuff of gods.

When the fire had grown strong enough, he added a small log from his wood pile that was in the shade of a nearby tree. The log crackled as the fire licked and evaporated the dew it had collected over the morning hours. As the fire grew in strength and size, consuming the log, he got up and walked over to where his breakfast was hanging. He untied the net bag and holding it in his hand, he reached up and pulled down a small, blackened pole that he had placed there for safekeeping.

The blackened pole was about three feet long. It was sharpened at both ends while over half its length was black with the fires and smoke of two years' worth of cooking. He brought his bag and his pole over to his cooking fire. He sat down on his log and pulled out his breakfast. The fish was big. Holding it over his legs, he took his pole and jammed it down the fish's throat. The pole slipped in through the dead animals' flesh with little problem and soon the sharpened black point of the pole was protruding about an inch out of its hind. That was a mistake. He would have to be careful that the fish did not slide down the pole. Why had he let the pole puncture through the fish? Had he been distracted?

With the fish held in place on the pole with his hand and his other held under the fish as a slide stop, he jammed the pole deep into the soft ground. The pole slid seven to eight inches into the ground, and he pulled it over the flames of his fire. The fish was at a good fifty-degree angle over the fire where the flames could not touch it. The flames licked at the thing especially when the fire drew forth the natural juices of its flesh, but the fish was held securely above the flames' hellish embrace.

Once he was satisfied with the setup and the progress of

his meal preparation he leaned down and grabbed his waterproof box. He opened it and took stock of his tinder. He would need to prepare a little more than usual. He had used more than he had wanted to build this fire. He always kept his tinder box full.

Except for that one time he had let his box run dangerously low. He had the foresight to stock up on dried meat and smoked fish. He was very cautious of how much dried food he stocked. He wasn't quite sure about how well that stuff really kept and out here there were no doctors or hospitals. If he got food poisoning, he would have to deal with it on his own. It rained for what seemed like a week straight. He was still so unused to the uncompromising environment that he had decided to stay in his burrow for the whole of that week, subsisting on his dried food stores. He woke up on the fourth or fifth day and realized that the rain had stopped. He decided to take the opportunity and go fishing while the weather held.

After some time, He was able to catch a fish and he brought it back to his kitchen clearing. He opened his tinder box and to his horror it didn't have near what he thought, and there was not enough inside to light the damp twigs and branches that he was able to gather from around the clearing. He had had to throw the fish away. He couldn't place at the time what he felt guiltier about, throwing away perfectly good food or having to miss out on a meal because he hadn't prepared. He spent that day shaving branches and gathering twigs and other kindling. He brought them back to his burrow which he placed around the ground and atop a log that he used as a chair so that they could dry. He went hungry for a few days and ever since he had made sure to keep his sizable tinder box full.

While his fish was cooking over the fire he got up and

walked into the forest. He found a good-sized branch from a pine tree. With his large knife, he cut it down and walked back to his clearing. He sat down sideways from his fire and began whittling and shaving the branch down making a nice little pile of shavings. He enjoyed this time of the morning. The sun was rising in the sky, his meal was cooking beside him, and he could enjoy the song of the forest. He inhaled the strong smell of cooking fish beside him mingled with the more earthy smells of the forest. This was the reason he had come out here in the first place.

He opened his tinder box, dumped what remained onto the log, and put the fresh pile of shaving into the bottom of the box, putting the older stuff on top. The box was not full to bursting, which was good, but more was better than less. He placed his flint stone and small red Swiss army knife inside, closed the waterproof seal on the box, and placed it inside his coyote skin bag.

He noticed that his fish was getting a little black on one side. He twisted the pole till the fish's other side was now facing the fire. The fish's juices ran down the blackened pole. Soon the fish would be ready to eat.

With his next day preparations done and his immediate chores taken care of, he reached back into his bag and pulled out another small box. This one was black and rectangular. He walked back into the forest. In the shade of the trees, he had dug out a small patch of earth and had placed a tarp inside the shallow hole. The tarp was placed to catch the morning dew for drinking and washing purposes.

He hunched down over the tarp and opened his black box. He pulled out his collapsible plastic cup and, filling it with the morning's harvest, drank the cool water. Once finished, he bent down and carefully gathered another cupful and set the cup down on the pine-needle-laden ground next to him.

He reached into his black box and pulled out a stick that was bigger than a twig but not nearly big enough for a branch. He dipped the stick into his cup of water and pulled a bright yellow box out from his black box. He hated this part of his morning. Flipping back the cover to the yellow box, he dipped the stick into it and allowed the moisture on the stick to pull away the white substance. Taking a deep breath, he jammed the stick into his mouth and began scrubbing his teeth. Even though he had been brushing his teeth like this for over a year, the baking soda had lost none of its bitter, salty taste. When he was done, he rinsed his mouth out with water. He placed the black box back in his bag, set his cup of water down next to him on his log, and watching the merry flame in front of him, waited for his fish to cook.

When he was satisfied that his fish was done, he rotated the cooking pole toward him and away from his fire. The fire was lower than it had been, and it was eating through the rest of the fuel. That was ok; he needed a bed of coals now, not a full fire. Inspecting the blackened fish, he took his knife out of its sheath and began scraping the dried blackened scales up and away from the body of the fish. He liked the sound his blade made as it caressed the blackened skin of his meal. As the scales made contact with the blade it sounded like chimes, subtle and soft. It was the closest thing to music that he could make, and he loved hearing his compositions. He indulged himself for a few more strokes; this served two purposes, getting rid of some of the inedible parts of the fish but it also gave the meat time to cool. Once he was satisfied with the fish, he ran the blade up through the stomach of the thing splitting it in half.

After some preparation he set one-half of the fish to smoke and, turning away from the smoke, he picked up the other half of his fish and began to eat. He had to be careful of the bones, he never really did a chef's job of deboning the things, but he was the one who was eating it. Besides, he didn't really have anything to debone the thing with anyway.

When he was done, he turned around to inspect the smoking of his fish. He decided to leave it there for a little longer and he gathered the bones of his finished meal. He walked back into the woods past his water reservoir and with his heel he dug out a small hole. He hunched down. He deepened the hole till it was three or four inches deep. He then dropped the bones into the earth and covered the hole.

Standing up, he rubbed his hands together; the juices of the fish and the scent of his meal were heavy on his hands. He walked back to his smoking fish. The smoke pillar was bigger than he remembered, and he knew that the black smoke would attract attention. He couldn't do anything about that now, not really. Besides, he had to survive too, and this was an essential part of his survival. He reached into his bag and pulled out yet another box. This one was about the shape and size of a shoebox. It was waterproof as well and it was a bright red, the bright crimson of blood.

His mind reached back to last night and he remembered the rich blood of the doe he had killed. Even though he was satisfied with his latest meal, his mouth began to water. There was something primal about the blood of animals that did something for him, something that he couldn't get anywhere else. It satisfied him in ways that fish and vegetables couldn't hope to equal.

Licking his lips, he opened the red box. Reaching into the smoke pillar he pulled out his fish half and placed it into the box. He closed the box and clasped it. He pulled the green branches from the fire. He fanned them into the air till they stopped smoking themselves and scattered them around the clearing. He extracted his cooking pole from the earth and stirred the coals, burying them with the dirt of the fire pit. Soon the smoke cleared, and the fire was nonexistent.

With pole in hand, he walked back to the tree with the rope hanging from it and replaced the pole next to the trunk of the tree. He grabbed hold of his rope and pulled himself an arm's length up it. He continued to climb up the short rope. It was only about six feet up, but he got a nice view of his clearing. He grabbed hold of the branch that the rope was fastened to and hung there for a while. His arms protested as he continued to hang in place. He allowed his muscles to work and felt the burning, sore sensation in his shoulders and forearms grow. He hung there till he decided that he had had enough and dropped down from the branch. His feet hit the ground, and the landing shockwave ran up his legs from his feet. It hurt a little, but a little pain never hurt anybody.

Isn't that what pain is?

Smiling at his own cleverness and idiocy, he walked back to his bag. He placed the red box inside his bag and checked around his kitchen area to see if anything was out of place. Seeing nothing, he grabbed his bag, fishing pole, and net bag.

He walked back to his burrow, keeping his head on a swivel, listening to the sounds of the forest around him. When he got home, he dropped the net and laid his fishing pole up against the great redwood. He placed his bag on the ground and opened the portal to his home. He picked up his bag and fishing pole, leaving his net on the ground.

He ducked inside his burrow, and he put his pole in its proper place. He placed his bag on the black bear skin of his bed and took one look around the place to ensure he had not been invaded by some rodents, spiders, snakes, or anything else. Laughing at his own sudden fear he shook his head and exited his home once more. You'd think after spending as much time out here as he had he wouldn't be so afraid to find one or two things that had freaked him out when he was a boy. But spiders still creeped him out and he had never been a great lover of snakes. And let's just say that rodents were rodents, and they were always unwelcome visitors.

Stepping outside once more he resealed his burrow. He reached down and grabbed his net bag and started back toward the river. The sun was just past its zenith in the sky and soon the forest would begin to darken with the shadows of late afternoon and dusk. Not being in any great hurry, he still decided to be a bit reckless and run. The cool forest air flowed into his lungs, and he could feel his blood begin to pump and his meal begin to be properly digested. The speed at which he could move now was greater than anything he had known while living in the civilized world and he let the air pass around him as he built speed running down the hillside. The dead pine needle carpet of the forest floor did not offer the best footing, but he was used to the uncertain terrain, and he allowed his feet to coast and slip over the needles. Running felt great but his human frame could not offer the sheer joy that he felt when he was able to run with his pack. His two legs offered none of the control, speed, or pure power of when he was able to run on four legs. When he was allowed by his Lunar Mother to do that, he felt all the power of a God and he knew what it was like to truly be alive. But human legs were all he had so he had to satisfy himself with all the limitations of this form and make the best of it.

He slowed down as he reached the river. His recklessness gone, he stopped and listened to the world around him as his blood beat loudly in his ears. He scanned the riverbanks and seeing nothing, stepped out. He approached the river and took off his vest and his pants. Seeing a calm eddy in the river he stepped into the frigid water. He dunked himself beneath the soft currents. His head exploded with the cold and his body went numb. He had to concentrate to keep from shouting as he jumped back up from the water. If he wasn't awake before he sure as hell was now. Shivering in the cool forest air with his lower body still submerged, he opened the net bag and dunked the net in the water, grabbing a handful of sand he began scrubbing it clean. Hunching down in the frigid current, he worked his shoulders and arms scrubbing the net. When he was done with it, he placed it on top of some rocks and submerged himself once more. The water was still bitterly cold, but he forced himself to stay under as he grabbed handfuls of sand and washed his body with the abrasive granules.

The water seemed to shrink his lungs and several times he had to surface and gulp more air. The cold seeped into his body. It was one of the hardships that didn't get any easier no matter how long he was here. The water was cold year-round. As he reached down for another handful of sand his hands wouldn't close properly and they were slow to open. This river posed threats just as deadly as any predator and he hurried with his bath.

He stood up and steam came off his goose-pimpled body. Reaching down again he grabbed another handful of sand and scrubbed his hair with it. He continued to scrub the rest of his body with sand. He submerged his body and, twisting in the water, he allowed the current to wash him clean again. Panting from the cold, he stepped up out of the water and jumped back into his warm animal skins. The warm fur was welcome after his frigid dip. He grabbed his net bag from their place on the rock. Taking a deep breath, he began to run up the hillside allowing his body to fight the cold that was threatening it. His blood pumped through his body and feeling returned to his numb fingers and toes. He continued to run as his blood carried warmth throughout his body. The mile or two uphill run was the best cure for the river water's frigid assault, and he was soon feeling warm again.

When he reached his burrow, he unsealed his portal and stepped inside. He breathed easier as the warmth of his burrow permeated his body. Even though he wasn't as cold as he was, he knew just how important body heat was to survival. Placing his net inside his coyote skin bag he laid down on his bed and covered himself with his bearskin blanket. The warm fur was always comforting, and he allowed the trapped heat under the fur to spread through his tired body.

3

He stared at his ceiling and smiled. This really was a good home and this place felt more like home to him than any other place he had ever lived. He let his thoughts drift back to his childhood. He had always been a little awkward and the fact that his parents moved around a lot didn't help him very much. He was attractive, yeah, but that was a detriment to him in most cases. Whenever he went to a new place, without fail, a gaggle of stupid girls would point him out and lower their heads together to giggle. He couldn't stand the sight of them. Of course, they would think he was cute, and that he was playing hard to get, so over the course of a week or two a parade of brightly clothed girls would come up and ask him if he thought this girl or that girl was cute. Then they would explain to him in hushed tones that whoever they had asked about thought he was cute. To be polite to these idiots, he would stand there and listen for several minutes about how their 'friend' was just so shy and wondered if he would ask her out.

"She really is a great girl, but she is just too shy to come up and ask you herself. You know, you really are cute. So, will you ask her out?"

After going through that ritual about five times in five different states he had learned to just kill the interrogations early. The result was that he had accumulated several reputations over the years. One was that he was an asshole, and that was the most common and usually the first. He began to hear other things as well, like that he was only interested in boys. He was mocked and had to endure hurled insults from people he had never met.

This was his life.

People didn't understand that he didn't want to get to know anybody because he would just have to leave them again. He had only finished a full year in the same school once. He had petitioned his parents several times about the prospect of being homeschooled. His dad thought that was actually a good idea but his mom, who had been a cheerleader in high school, was adamant about keeping him in school because the social skills that he would build in school were essential to a healthy lifestyle. She wasn't ready to admit that moving from place to place and starting over once, twice, and in one school year, three times, wasn't building any social skills anyway. After his freshman year of high school, his mom gave in and began his homeschooling program.

Wow. Mom. If you could see your 'little angel' now. What would you do if you knew that I was out here in the wilderness and those social skills you kept forcing down my throat were completely useless to me?

He threw the bearskin off his body and sat up. He reached into his dresser and grabbed his whetstone. Unsheathing his knife, he began to sharpen his weapon. He drew the stone down the blade's edge. He was bored; he could admit it and the rhythmic scraping sound of the stone upon the steel always calmed him for some reason. He drew the stone along the edge in a practiced stroke. The burrow did allow in some light though it was always dark, a perpetual dusk that never seemed to lift fully from his sanctuary out in the middle of the harsh expanses of nature. The soft scraping sound echoed off his walls and he let his shoulders and arms work the blade.

Once the blade was sharp, he sheathed it and stood up. How long had he been in here? Stepping over to his portal he unsealed the door and stepped out into the dusk of his forest. He must have fallen asleep, no wonder it had been so dark in his burrow.

Closing and resealing his portal he walked toward his kitchen area taking a circular path to help cover his passing and make it just a little harder for any predator to track him. He walked uphill and switched back away from his kitchen. He started downhill and cut to his right and he turned toward his burrow once more. He walked in the random serpentine pattern for a while and soon the sun's light was barely traceable in the deep forest. He quickened his pace and came upon his kitchen clearing.

It looked exactly the way it had when he had left this morning. He hurried across the open space, careful not to step on one of the branches he had scattered there earlier. He scanned his surroundings. The night was still, and his Lunar Mother had taken her place on her throne. He looked upon her heavenly glory. She was still plump, but she wasn't full. A good-sized shaving on her side had been taken out and she looked lopsided. Even with that small imperfection showing she was still beautiful. He felt privileged to be able to look upon her and know that she was confident enough in herself to show with unflinching pride that she at times was imperfect, just like he was.

The sky had been invaded by a few puffy clouds. Nothing that foretold of a storm, but the clouds were an unwelcome visitor for his mother and the stars that attended her. He lowered his eyes and thanked her for her blessings that had allowed him to truly live a night or two ago. He was very good at telling at least the number of days that had passed since the last time his mother had been full. But sometimes he was a little iffy, and he wasn't sure if two days had passed or only one.

Feeling the hairs on the back of his neck rise, he whipped around drawing his blade free and holding it at the ready. Even in the moonlight, he could see well. He scanned as deep into the forest as he could. Every nerve ending was taught, and his breathing had quickened. He turned around in a full circle, scanning the trees. If there was something out there, he couldn't see it. He glanced up into the tree branches as they shone with the white light of the moon. A soft wind passed by, and the tree branches swayed with the movement. Keeping his knife at the ready, he left his clearing and headed for his burrow.

Something wasn't right.

He couldn't shake the feeling that something was watching him. His forest had eyes that were watching him at all times, but this was a little more pressing than that. He hadn't felt anything like this since this morning when he had found the black she-wolf watching him from the far riverbank. But before that, had he ever felt this? Had he ever felt it like this, this desperate? Keeping his head rotating and his feet moving he couldn't remember when or if he had ever felt like this. There was something he was supposed to do or something he was supposed to see, and his stupid human senses were not allowing him to see whatever it was his instincts were telling him to see.

He was feeling his way through his woods now more than seeing the underbrush. He had walked the woods at night and his feet found the clear path through the roots and bushes. The moonlight was still bright enough for him to cast a shadow when her light was allowed to reach the forest floor. The feeling that something was watching him seemed to be growing with every step. His heart began to beat so loudly he had trouble listening to the sounds around him. This is what a snow hare felt like just before the snow wolf attacked. He was now almost in a blind panic. All he could think of was getting back to the safety of his burrow.

The shadows of the forest began to take on menacing shapes and he began to see predators and killers next to every tree. Every bush he brushed up against hid a venomous viper or rattlesnake. Every branch he walked under supported some hideous spider hanging from its disgusting web, waiting to drop down and bite him, eager to inject its venom into his unprotected neck. He wasn't concentrating on anything. All he could feel was his fear. It had taken hold of him. He hadn't felt fear like this possibly ever and it was going to kill him, he knew, but he could not get control of it and the panic had a firm hold on his mind.

Almost blind, he stumbled over a bush and fell face-first onto the pine-needle-strewn ground. The earthy smell that he had become so used to over the past year and a half seemed so comforting. He allowed his hands to reach out and grab hold of the earth. The smell of home relaxed him, and he breathed deeply the perfume of the forest. The solid earth that he dragged from its place with his fingers felt so wonderful, it was tangible, and that simple feeling of earth evaporated the shadows that had robbed him of his senses.

He closed his eyes and forced his heart to slow, and he listened to his forest. The gentle song of the forest was absent. The birds did not sing. He realized that he had not yet heard the howl of a wolf or coyote.

His forest was silent.

He concentrated on the lack of music around him and then, from the silence around him he heard it. It was very faint and still far off, but it was there. Carried on the back of the wind, so faint he wasn't surprised that he had missed it in his panic, were the voices of people.

What would people be doing here? They couldn't be hunters. They were being too loud for that. The sound of their voices carried up from the west. His burrow was to the west, but only about a thousand feet maybe.

He stood. The feeling of being watched had disappeared and the fear was completely gone from his system. He crouched down and moved through the forest like a predator hunting his prey. He moved through the under-brush, the whisper of his feet as they stepped on the soft pine needles was the only sound he made. He slid from shadow to shadow as he used the trees for protection. The forest was his home and the men he sought were in his back yard. He crouched next to a large redwood. He looked out through the forest and saw the harsh beams of man-made flashlights cut through the beauty of the night like a razor and it dimmed everything around them. There were quite a few of them. The beams did a great job of illuminating what they were pointing at, but if he could avoid the direct beams, they wouldn't be able to see him.

Staying low to the ground he moved closer. He could count about ten or twelve beams with more being turned on and off at irregular intervals. What in the hell was going on? Using the shadows as his armor he moved closer. He could hear the voices more clearly. They were not trying to be quiet. He was becoming irritated at the lack of respect these men showed the night and to his forest. There was a lot of harsh yelling, and he could hear the roar of some motor. The brightest white light he had seen in years erupted into the night, illuminating the forest, and effectively blinding him.

He turned back to the safety of his tree's shadow, and he closed his eyes to clear the retinal burn from his eyes. Keeping his eyes closed, he listened to what the people were yelling at each other. He couldn't hear much over the roar of the engine that was powering the bright flood lights that had just blinded him, but he did catch a little of what was going on.

"This is a nice little shelter," he heard one male voice say.

That is not just a shelter asshole! It's my home!

Having some vision restored he peeked around his tree into the bright light. He could clearly see that there were at least twenty people out there. There were several guys with long trench coats, holding steaming cups of what was probably coffee. He couldn't be sure, but he was fairly certain that they were cops of some sort. There were little groups of them standing around yelling at each other over the loud machinery. He couldn't make out anything specific but the expression on some of their faces was a mixture of mirth and exasperation.

He leaned back into the shadows and rested his head on the tree's great trunk. This was his mom's fault. It was the only possible explanation. She had finally found him. He didn't know how but somebody somewhere had pointed them in his direction. *Mom, why are you doing this to me?* He knew that she was probably just worried about him, and she had probably spent a lot of sleepless nights crying over his 'disappearance.' That thought was sobering.

He leaned out around his trunk and watched the unwelcome visitors. He saw people dressed in full-body white plastic suits begin to come out of his burrow. He hadn't seen these people before. What were they doing wearing hazmat suits out in the middle of the woods? They were each carrying suitcase-looking things of various sizes and as they exited his burrow his spirits dropped. The suitcase things probably held his stuff, his clothes, and his coyote skin bag with all his precious boxes inside namely the red one that still held his leftover fish.

His stomach crunched and grumbled at the thought of the food that was being taken away from him. What were they doing? And why did they need the carrying cases? There were quite a few of them and he knew that his burrow had been cleaned out. Even if he could get over there, there wouldn't be anything left for him to grab. He saw one officer grab the arm of a hazmat-suited guy. The officer was yelling something at the guy and the guy tried to turn away. The officer used his leverage to wrench the hazmat suit guy back around to face him. Another guy, who he hadn't noticed before, came out of nowhere and leveled a nightstick across the officer's face, dropping him. He winced as he could hear the crunch of flesh from where he crouched in the shadows. The guy with the nightstick looked out over the rest of the group of cops and turned to follow the parade of hazmat suit guys up the hillside. Two officers ducked down and helped the assaulted officer back to his feet. The officer dusted himself off and massaged his jaw. The two that had helped him to his feet shook their heads looking back and forth between the assaulted officer and the retreating assailant. They were yelling something, but he couldn't make out anything clearly. He watched as another officer started wrapping crime scene tape around a fairly big area that enclosed his burrow.

Staying in the shadows of the trees, he began his retreat from the scene. He was cautious of his footing but also of the bright light that burned behind him. Like a frog using lily pads to get across a pond, he used the shadows of the trees to make good his escape from these invading people. He was a wraith, unseen by men, and fast. He soon left the commotion of the scene behind him, and he began to breathe easier.

As he walked his mind worked on the problem. How to survive without any of his gear? He didn't think he could. He had learned so much living with the forest but the tools that he had brought with him were essential to that purpose. The thought of his kitchen area struck him, and he started to run, silent and swift like the shadows themselves.

If the cops had found him out here in the wilderness, then they wouldn't leave without finding as much as they could. The place didn't seem like home anymore. The birds weren't singing. No wolves or coyotes howled. He ran, his long strides eating distance, separating him from the invaders.

He skirted around the edge of his kitchen clearing, staying hidden within the shadows of the trees. He ran around the perimeter of the clearing, using all his senses to ensure he was alone. The gentle light of his Lunar Mother flooded the clearing, and he could see as clearly as if it were day. His kitchen looked the same as it had when he had left it this morning. He continued to move around the perimeter of the clearing till he reached his water reservoir tarp.

He picked up the clear plastic and shook out the water that had collected there. He was probably going to need that, but he didn't have any time. For all he knew the cops had brought dogs to track him and the dogs would have all the scent they needed from invading his burrow. He smiled at the thought of suing a cop for breaking and entering. His door had been closed and they hadn't shown him a warrant and what had he done to deserve to be arrested anyway? Those were the thoughts of a child, and he wasn't playing a game. If being happy out here in his forest meant that he had to hide from the cops as well as his mother, then he wished them luck. Humans were frail and he had become stronger than he had ever dreamed possible from his time out here. And he was sure that no human or groups of humans could possibly catch him. As he was folding his tarp into a square that he would be able to carry, he heard another sound that was alien to him. It was loud and rhythmic. His eyes widened in horror as he realized it was a helicopter. If they had brought in a helicopter, they meant to have him even if they had to capture him and bring him in like a criminal.

Placing the folded tarp on the ground he pulled out his knife and began digging in the soft ground. Of course, it would never occur to these people that he liked living out here and he didn't want to go back. No, they wouldn't understand that nor would his mother. The leftover fish that he had left in his burrow gave them all the evidence they needed to prove that he was alive. If he hadn't left that evidence behind, maybe he could have evaded them long enough for them to conclude that he had died somewhere in the forest, and they were unable to recover his body. But that was wishful thinking.

As he dug down deeper, he fell into a rhythm of stab, stab, stab, and shovel with his free hand. Stab, stab, stab, shovel with his free hand.

The sound of the helicopter dominated the night. He could tell that it was still far off, but he knew that it was going to find him in this clearing if he didn't hurry. His knife chinked at what he had been looking for. He wiped the dirt off his blade and sheathed it. He grabbed at the dirt with both hands and pulled the earth away till he could pull out what he had been looking for. He almost couldn't believe that it was still here. Burying this had been one of the first things he had done when he found this clearing.

He brushed away the dirt and looked at his old tin lunchbox. The GI Joe insignia on the top of the box was faded and he couldn't quite make out what, or who, was on the front. The box was rusted badly but he knew that would be the case. He unclasped the locks and pried the rusted lid open. The hinges of the tin box snapped with a loud metallic ring and the box flew open in his hands.

He ripped the tape holding the plastic bag to the bottom of the tin. He looked at the bag and sighed. He opened the bag and pulled out the smaller bag inside. He held the bag up to the light and thanked himself for having the foresight to plan this contingency. He looked into the bag and the green bills with the large number one hundred on them were still intact. He shoved the bag into the inside pocket of his vest that he had sewn there when he made the thing. He had never needed pockets out here but back then the habit of having a pocket was so great that he had sown it into the skin vest, just another small thing that he had decided to do back then, for no real reason, that he was praising himself for now.

He could hear the helicopter as the rotor blades grew louder and he knew that he had run out of time. Patting the pocket with his hand he took off running. He knew that he would have to put as much distance between himself and

the helicopter as possible. He knew a little bit about helicopter and cop search patterns. They would start at his
burrow and slowly work their way out in a circular pattern.
With the helicopter taking point it would be the real eyes of
the search party and soon cops would be all over this clearing. The hanging rope and the manicured stump that he
had spent so many hours sitting on would point to him
having been there as clearly as if he had left road signs.

The fear of the predators of this place was not so much
his concern now. The sound of the helicopter and the
disturbance of all the people traipsing through the forest in
the middle of the night would do all he needed it to do to
keep the forest clear and predators at bay, for a time at least.

He crashed through the forest. He wasn't concerned with
stealth so much as speed and he ran as fast as his legs would
carry him. He kicked up pine needles as his toes gripped the
earth with each stride. The wind rushing past him was
contesting with the sound of the helicopter for dominance
over his hearing and he found himself smiling. Even now,
being hunted as he was, with adrenaline pumping and
blood flowing freely through his veins. He was truly alive.

He concentrated on the ground and the trees. There was
nothing else, even the sound of the wind and the hunting
helicopter faded from his consciousness. All there was in his
universe was the ground, the trees, and his running.
Nothing else existed.

He reached the river and slowed. He listened and
studied the sound of the helicopter. It seemed to be far
behind him, but the sound was changing and seemed to be
making a regular beating pattern. The helicopter was
circling. It had found his kitchen and was studying it
making several passes around it. It was the only logical
explanation. Studying that place meant that they weren't

coming down the hill yet and that meant that he could cross the river in relative safety.

He ran upstream till he found the shallow ford that he had used many times and ran across. His legs kicked up great sprays of water and made a lot of noise. The water cooled and massaged his feet as they slammed down into the surface of the moving water and gripped the smooth rock bed. His toes spread and he had good footing as he crossed the river and clambered up the opposing riverbank.

Once on dry land he turned back to face southward and listened to the helicopter. It was still making the same beating pattern it had a moment ago. The helicopter was still circling but the beats of the pattern were getting longer and slower. He knew that the helicopter was widening its search radius. It would take them a long time to reach the river at this pace, but he also knew that he couldn't outrun a helicopter. He turned northward and began to run up the opposite hillside.

He let his well-conditioned leg muscles carry him up the hill past the remains of the deer carcass he had shared with his pack the last full moon. Her skeleton gleamed in the soft moonlight that filtered down through the trees. The skeleton was in good shape, and it was very clean. After he had run with his wolves' other animals must have come to finish the meal. Maybe coyotes, maybe other smaller rodents, probably a combination of both.

Leaving the carcass behind he continued to run uphill. He hadn't had any real clear idea about where he was going but his legs were carrying him on a familiar path. If the helicopter was circling it could close the distance between itself and him very quickly. He hated that damn machine that beat nature into submission with its rotor blades. By all laws of physics, the helicopter shouldn't be able to fly. The flight dynamics of an airplane working in harmony with natural air currents were absent when discussing a helicopter. The blades spun till the air itself was forced to lift the damn thing off the ground. That was what he had come to expect of people. Why live or act in harmony with something when you could just beat it till it served in the way that you wanted it to?

He found himself on the ridgeline of his valley. He stopped and took in his surroundings, allowing the burning sensation in his tired leg muscles to relax and rest for a short time. He looked south over his valley. He saw the tiny helicopter in the distance with its bright beam of artificial light shooting out of the underside like a lightsaber, cutting through the curtain of night as cleanly as a razor blade through butter. He could make out some other small lights making their way clumsily through the trees.

He knelt over the rock that made up this high part of the valley. He stroked the cool rock surface and rested his hand on the rough mineral. This valley had been his home for so long and now he was being forced out. He leaned over and rested his head on the rock face. He closed his eyes and there, within full sight of his Lunar Mother, two single tears dropped from his eyes. They made an infinitesimally small splash, and he breathed in a deep ragged breath.

"Mother, please forgive me."

He prayed for the loss of his home and his pack. He asked for forgiveness for not being strong enough to do what was necessary. He asked to be forgiven for allowing these invaders to take what they wanted and to do as they pleased with no regard for the natural laws that he had lived by for close to two years. He asked for forgiveness for having to leave his valley and all those that he had protected behind.

He lifted himself up and looked south again. The tears were gone from his eyes but the pain of seeing that machine in the air didn't hurt any less. He stood up in one fluid motion and looked around his present location. He knew this place. This was where he had been blessed by his mother a few nights ago. He spun around and scanned the rock. He shifted and walked a few steps, scanning the ground. He trotted a few steps forward then back again. His head moved to the right and left while his well-attuned eyes took in every detail of the curvature of the rock and the folds and the dirt that had collected in the crevices of the rock face. He turned around once more, and his eyes found what he was looking for. He knelt and scooped up half a pair of his denim shorts. These were his shorts that had ripped when he changed. But this was only one-half. He would need to find the other half. He wasn't going to leave a bread-crumb for these cops to follow. He wanted his trail cold and stale by morning.

He continued to search the area in a circular pattern from where he had found the first piece of his shorts. The rock in this small area seemed to be rougher than the area he had just come from. As a result, more dirt and moss were growing in the crevices of the rock face. He reached down for what at first looked like the other half of his shorts, but his hand closed around a clump of dense moss. He kept looking.

He was exposed on the rock face. He knew that his time was short, but he wasn't going to leave without the evidence of his missing clothes. He looked for the other half of his denim shorts.

With little warning, he was suddenly bathed in a pool of purest white light and was deafened by a roar of wind and a terrible sound that drowned out everything else.

4

William threw up his arm to protect his eyes from the blinding white light that now surrounded him. He stumbled to the left and sat down heavily on the rock face.

The helicopter was talking to him, something about not running, agents would apprehend him, and something about 'shoot to kill.' He had a hard time focusing on the voice over the roar of the rotor blades above him, and the pressure of the wind caused by the rotor wash. He felt the wind force increase, and his sense of hearing was even more drowned out as the helicopter lowered itself closer to him.

His eyes saw very little except the retinal burn from the bright light. But out of the corner of his eyes, he was able to see the bushes and trees moving, and not from the rotor wash of the helicopter. *Those agents are quick.*

William shook his head and with blind rage, he threw himself onto all fours kicking off the rock face. Using the momentum from that he picked himself up and ran blindly toward the far clearing. If these cops or whoever they were wanted him, they would have to shoot him. He thought he felt, more than heard, a bullet ricochet off the rock close to him. The hairs on the back of his neck stood up as he felt a presence come up from behind him. He forced himself to run faster.

What was behind him darted out in front of him. It was a wolf. Its black fur reflected the white light as it darted ahead of William. The wolf dove headfirst into the bushes and disappeared. William didn't have any choice, but if a wolf went in that direction, then the odds of other people being there were almost nonexistent. William plunged after the wolf and dove into the bushes, rolling on his shoulder and resting behind the trunk of a pine tree.

The helicopter followed William and the wolf, sweeping its searchlight over the trees, trying to penetrate the tight canopy of the trees. William stayed where he was and from the safety of the shadows, watched the helicopter's flood light illuminate the forest all around him. He hid himself behind the large tree. He watched as the flood light pivoted and swung back and forth all around him with its harsh light.

A wet rough texture pushed against his arm. Startled, he looked down. The wolf was pressing its face into his hand. Having some time to actually look at the wolf, he now saw that it was the she-wolf who had been watching him in the river earlier that day, the mostly black with a white starburst on her chest, and hanging in her mouth was the piece of denim shorts he had been looking for.

He reached down to grab the fabric and the wolf backed away a quick two steps, just out of his reach. He stepped away from the protection of the tree he was hiding behind and took a step toward the wolf. She turned and trotted off several feet away. There was nothing he could do but follow the animal. When the wolf saw that he was following her, she began to trot west through the tree line, going neither uphill nor downhill. The wolf wound her way through the trees, avoiding the sweeping beams of light from the helicopter. William was careful to follow in her steps.

He followed the she-wolf at a jog. The sound of the helicopter's rotor blades were fading, still loud, but not as menacing as it had been before. He looked to the north, and he could still see the flood light through the trees, but it was searching in a circular pattern, not following directly after them.

The she-wolf trotted between the trees, almost hopping from one tree shadow to the next. She was following a pattern that he had used when he was retreating from the cops and his burrow.

The helicopter must have turned around because the sound was quickly diminishing, faster than he and the wolf were moving through the forest. That was good but where was she taking him? She was still trotting from shadow to shadow going farther west toward the ocean. The ground beneath his feet was cold with the dew of the early morning. He had no idea what time it was, but he knew the sun would rise in a few hours.

He couldn't see the moon, so he couldn't get a clear idea about the time. The wolf seemed oblivious to his presence, and he needed to recover the shorts that still hung from her jaws.

He continued to chase after the animal, and he slipped from shadow to shadow in her wake. She was graceful and fluid in her movements as if she knew with exacting precision what muscle to move and when. Her trot was well-balanced and easy. She far surpassed the jumpy trot of any dog. As he followed her west, he wondered where they were going. He had never been this far west. He had always assumed that his pack lived on this north side of the valley, and he had never dared to wander too far when he was to transform.

The realization struck him. *She's taking me to her den.* The thought of coming face to face with a den full of wolves without being transformed froze him with terror and he stopped still in the shadow of a large tree.

The she-wolf didn't take long to realize that her charge was no longer following her. She came to a graceful stop and turned around. She trotted back to him. The piece of denim was still hanging from her jaws, and she pushed his leg with her nose. He bent his leg with the pressure but didn't move. Since moving to this forest, he had lost much of his fear and uncertainty; but a den full of wolves was an encounter he could not survive. Running full speed into that situation wasn't courage, it was a death wish, which he didn't have.

The wolf pressed against him again and when his leg bent, she growled. A low, dangerous, and primal sound that at once made him look down at her. Her lips were pulled back from her jaws, and he could see her teeth as they ripped deeper into what was left of his denim shorts. Her eyes were glaring at him over her nose. He eased his hand to the knife its sheath, ready to draw it at a moment's need. The wolf seemed to be watching his hands because she growled louder and pushed his leg again.

What did this animal want? Where was she leading him? These questions crowded into his mind, and he wasn't able to think clearly. Was her den where she was leading him to? These thoughts jockeyed for position in his mind, and, in his mental anguish, he forgot to hold his ground and found himself being moved and pushed by the she-wolf. She was not going to take 'no' for an answer.

CHRISTOPHER SCHERRER

The she-wolf trotted ahead of him, and they resumed their pace. He could barely make out the sound of the helicopter now, and he knew that for the moment he was safe from his human pursuers. His animal escort, and wherever she was taking him, was a different story.

As he followed her, he began to wonder if they were going to go all the way to the ocean. He didn't have to wonder for long because the wolf turned to the north and headed up toward the ridge line of the valley.

The sky was getting lighter. He didn't feel tired, but he knew that he would need to rest soon. They came out of the trees, and he looked out over his valley. A fog had rolled in from the ocean and the whole bottom of his valley was covered in a thick white blanket of mist that his eyes could not penetrate. He smiled at the thought of successfully eluding those agents, or military, or whoever they were. But the smile slid from his face. He eluded them for one night but if they had found him here, they would find him anywhere. Was he to be a hunted animal for the rest of his life?

As he looked out over his valley and pondered his options, he felt a now familiar pressure against his legs. He looked out over what had been his home for nearly two years and began to think about where he would live now.

A sharp pain ran up through his leg. He jerked his head down staring at the wolf with shock and surprise. The wolf had backed up a step or two and he could swear she was smiling at him, his denim shorts still hanging from her mouth. *She just bit me. What a bitch!* He reached down and inspected his pants for damage.

"Why the hell did you do that?"

The mostly black-furred she-wolf stared back at him. The she-wolf seemed to stick her nose in the air as she turned around and trotted north toward the top of the valley. He followed, grumbling at being bitten by this animal.

They crested the ridge line. The terrain on this side of the ridge was a lot rockier and harder on his feet than the pine-needle-strewn ground of his valley. He was thankful for the easy pace that the wolf stayed at, and he was struck again by the question of where exactly they were going.

The mountainous terrain they now traveled left them exposed with no cover at all. If the helicopter came back anytime soon, they would be spotted. He climbed up the loose rock-strewn boulders. While he was breathing heavily with the effort, he looked up and watched the she-wolf leap over the terrain with no difficulty at all. Not for the first time he wished he could transform into his werewolf form at will, then he could show the little wolf how it was done. But as he was it was all he could do just to keep up with the four-legged she-devil.

As they climbed higher, he felt the cold wind coming off the ocean, chilling him through his exertion. Soon, winter would make its way to this part of the world, but it would not come for another moon or two. Here on the exposed elevated rocks, he could feel the wind cut through his clothes and his hands began to go numb. The she-wolf was oblivious to these environmental changes, because she just kept leaping from boulder to boulder going ever higher and northward. He had followed the animal this far, and she was leading him somewhere. Where that somewhere was, was a different question altogether.

He followed the wolf down into a slight dip in the mountains. They followed this easier terrain east away from the ocean. The crevice was sharp, and he had to jump from one side to the other to avoid his feet getting caught in the sharp rocks. The she-wolf picked up her pace and jumped to the other side of the crevice. He almost laughed out loud. They were performing team figure eights. Alternating who was on the north and south sides of the crevice then they would switch places. It became a game for him to see how perfectly he could mirror the she-wolf's movements. For a time, it was fun. He felt the pure joy of life that he had experienced so often in the last year and a half, and he was happy.

In that moment, the sun crested over the mountain and the crevice in which they were trotting was flooded with the warm bright sunlight of the new day. The rays of the sun were a welcome relief from the night's cold wind and the stone over which they now ran. He felt warmth press down on him and through him and he could feel his feet begin to warm. The rock was still cold, but he knew that his hands and feet would be warm soon enough.

As he trotted with the she-wolf he heard his stomach growl. He hadn't eaten in a while, and he was beginning to feel it. The she-wolf might be able to go days without eating but people worked a little differently.

They continued to trot along the crevice at an even pace neither hurrying nor slowing. As the morning wore on, he began to feel an uncomfortable warmth building on the soles of his feet. It had been so long since he had walked on stone or any surface that held heat. His feet were not used to it, and he found himself jumping from one side of the crevice to another faster than the she-wolf was just to bring some relief to his burning feet.

The two escapees continued their way along the crevice. It wasn't a question of why he was following the wolf so much as where the wolf was leading him. As he allowed his mind to work on that quandary, he almost missed the fact that the crevice they followed was bottoming out and instead of a sharp bottom, it had gradually become flat. He dropped down and began to run along the flat bottom of the crevice just as the wolf was doing. They were able to move faster and again he heard his stomach growl in protest.

The sun had reached its zenith in the sky, and he was now weak with hunger. He had to stop and rest. The wolf ran onward as he slowed and rested his arm on the wall of the crevice. His head lowered as he gasped for air. His lungs didn't seem to want to fill properly, and he was dizzy. He was not just leaning on his arm, but he was supporting his entire weight with his arm. He couldn't keep trotting like this. His feet burned and he was hungry to the point of having a headache. That was something he didn't miss about civilization. He hadn't suffered a headache since being out in the wild. Now it seemed like the ailment wanted to make up for lost time. The pain racked his head from the inside out and his vision blurred. He moved his tongue around the inside of his very dry mouth. He hadn't had anything to drink in a very long time. All these things plus, he assumed, the altitude and the lack of shade was working very hard to sap him of all his strength.

The elements were winning.

He closed his eyes against the thunderous pain that throbbed inside his head. He just wanted to go to sleep. He had been up for so long with only a nap to sustain him. He let his legs fold underneath him and he slid down to sit inside the crevice. His wolf guide was forgotten for the time being and he was happy to rest. With his eyes shut against the harsh glare of the sun and warm rock radiating heat through his fur vest and pants, he smiled as he felt himself drift off to sleep.

A rough, wet texture pressed against his face and hands. The sensation tickled, but he didn't want to open his eyes, he wanted to keep sleeping. The sensation became more of a pressing and nudging and he tried to push it away. His hand pushed up against soft, warm thick fur and his eyes shot open. He was inside the crevice that he had followed a she-wolf into the night before. The wolf was pressing into him with her nose urging him to move. She had been licking his face and he saw the piece of denim that she had carried with her all night lying on the warm rock bed close by.

He allowed her to help him to his feet. He was more than a little groggy and he found it difficult to keep his balance. He put his hand on the crevice wall to steady himself and pulled it away from the hot surface. His legs didn't want to respond and when he took the first step, he had to catch himself before he fell flat on his face. His headache had not gone away, and he was even thirstier now than he was before he went to sleep. It was his own fault he knew. *Never fall asleep in the sunlight. It just makes you more dehydrated than you were before.* He had learned that from some people who lived out in the desert, back when he was still living in the land of normal civilized people.

The wolf had already picked up the piece of denim and was walking ahead of him keeping a wary eye on her charge. If this wolf actually cared about him, and he believed she did, then she was truly a remarkable creature and he found himself wondering what he had done to deserve the nurturing care of a she-wolf. He stumbled forward as his legs and feet remembered how to work again and he followed his guide.

They moved at a slower pace. His whole being protested moving at all, and it was all he could do just to keep moving. The wolf was not oblivious to his drop in energy, and she contented herself to steadily keep only a few steps ahead of him.

He came to the realization that the crevice they had been traveling had been widening. He also realized that it was now slanted downhill. The sun was well past its zenith and soon the high walls of the crevice would cover them in shadow. He silently thanked the goddess for the anticipated reprieve from the heat of the sun, even though he knew that the stone would hold the sun's heat for a time. His feet would get some respite from the burning surface. He sighed gratefully and continued to follow his four-legged guide.

They continued to follow the crevice. The sun slipped out of sight and shadow covered him. He saw the harsh line between light and shade displayed sharply on the rock wall. The crevice must have changed direction and instead of traveling east, they were now traveling north.

How long would he follow her? That question was not something he had thought of before that moment. He had started by wanting to get that piece of denim back from her. He had followed her out of danger and out of his valley. He had followed her into the mountains and now at the point of exhaustion, he followed in her footsteps. Why?

A piece of evidence that he wanted concealed from the authorities could answer one or two of those questions but not all of them.

Why was he following her?

He didn't have a good answer except he had an instinctual urge to follow her. The she-wolf was obviously aware of his physical limitations. She maintained his speed, not hers. She had come back and awoken him from his nap in the crevice. She was very deliberate in how she made him understand to follow her last night. This was a very special wolf. She had intelligence and an awareness that some scientists might describe as an evolutionary step for the species.

He laughed out loud to himself. Who was he kidding? He was no scientist and besides her behavior could just be that of a mother. Had he been adopted by a she-wolf? The thought was almost too ridiculous to entertain. He couldn't keep a straight face as he allowed his laughter to echo off the walls of the rock. The she-wolf looked over her shoulder, the piece of denim still secured in her jaws. The look she gave him if she had been human would have been one of puzzlement and perhaps exasperation. Wolves felt emotion, but giving human explanations to wolf emotions was something he had always scoffed at. And now look at him, describing a wolf with human traits and quirks. He shook his head and snickered at his own stupidity. The wolf turned back around and continued to walk on.

As the sun's shadow line disappeared from the crevice entirely the wolf turned sharply and followed another shallow crevice. The mountainous rock was not barren here. Over the shallow walls of this new path, he could see colors, some dirt, and off in the distance he could just make out the top of trees. He could have cried. Trees meant food and shelter but most importantly, they meant water.

The copse of trees seemed to be the wolf's destination and they walked directly toward them. He supported himself on the rock as twilight settled. The old man must have already lost his battle with the ocean and soon the cold night of autumn would be fully upon them. The wind seemed to pick up speed now that they were outside the protective walls of the deep crevice that they had followed and soon he was shivering. The wolf seemed to sense this and pressed herself against his deerskin pants. He could feel her warmth through the fur of his pants, and he was grateful for it.

They walked toward the trees. The she-wolf's strength aided him in his strides, and he let her help support him. The night seemed to come faster than he anticipated, and he could see all the stars of the heavens with a clear view that he had lacked deep inside his valley. The stars were splashed against the blue-black backdrop of night. The goddess's brush had made a thick swath of dense stars through the middle of the sky and all the stars were there watching him. The moon was smaller tonight than she had been yesterday. It was always thus, the moon had her phases and she moved as the natural order of things dictated. Even if he spent every night and every day of his life without sleeping, he would never be able to count the multitude of lights that inhabited this sky. Even now, exhausted almost beyond his human capacity, his heart lifted. His spirits rose to meet those stars in the heavens, and he was filled with deep contentment and joy.

"Thank you, for allowing me to see and appreciate the beauty that still exists in this world," William whispered.

His guide led him closer to the trees. He was surprised at just how many there were. This was a small forest, not just a lone clump of a handful of trees. As the wolf led him deeper into the trees he felt at home. He inhaled and he could smell cedar pines and redwoods. The pine needle floor was a welcome relief to his feet, and he found his gait strengthening. The wolf led him to a clearing and he collapsed on the ground. The she-wolf watched him as he rested on the ground. Keeping the piece of denim in her mouth, she ran off into the woods.

He was left alone, exhausted and disoriented. His head

throbbed softly with the dull pain of his headache that didn't show any signs of lessening.

He studied his surroundings. The trees smelled similar, and the pale moonlight filtered through them in much the same way that he was accustomed to. He didn't know if the wolf was going to be back and he was too exhausted to hunt even if he had the right weapons, which he didn't. He unsheathed his knife and stood up.

The wind had ebbed as he was protected by the surrounding trees, but he needed to think about shelter and staying warm through the night. He began to gather wood for a fire. He searched around the clearing for various sticks and pieces of wood. He was able to find a good supply of dried, dead wood on the ground and didn't need to do much cutting. He gathered the various pieces of fuel into a nice pile and went out again for another load. Once he was satisfied that the amount of wood would last him through the night, he went looking for water.

He walked deeper into the forest, and he found what he was looking for. A clear, brisk-moving stream. The water didn't look deep, but it looked cold as it happily bubbled and gurgled over the various rocks of the creek bed. He followed it downstream a good distance and staying a safe distance away from the creek, he relieved himself. He hadn't had a bowel movement in over a day and his body was not happy with him. Fighting through constipation, he finished and cleaned himself with sand from the creek bed.

He put his pants back on and walked back upstream. He leaned over the water and drank straight from the creek. The cold crisp water lowered his core temperature a few degrees, but it did wonders for his energy levels. He felt a little more alive, a little stronger but also ready to sleep.

He walked back to the clearing. He didn't have to worry about double backing and covering his tracks. He knew that the she-wolf was going to be back, and she would be leading him away from these woods soon. Something told him this was not their destination and, not for the first time, he wondered where exactly she might be taking him.

Once he got back to the clearing, he cut a good, strong, green branch from a nearby tree and sat down next to his wood pile. Taking his knife and some pieces of wood he gathered previously, he shaved off a good amount of kindling and shavings for tinder. As he worked, he kept his ears alert, listening to the sounds of this unfamiliar place. It was dangerous to not pay attention to your surroundings, especially since he was a visitor here. When he had a good amount of tinder piled up, he took up the green branch he had cut down. Placing it off to one side he took out his half of his denim shorts and cut a strip of material from it.

Taking the strip, he tied it to one end of the green branch. Putting that end of the branch into the ground he bent the stick until he could tie the other end of the denim to the other end of the stick. It took him one or two tries. The strip of denim was not as long as he would have liked but he had to make do with what he had. Once his makeshift bow was completed, he grabbed a good-sized half branch and split the thing down the middle. Once he had a good flat piece of wood to work with, he took his knife and dug out a small depression in the log.

He had to stop for a moment. This was hard work and with his body already exhausted, he didn't know if he even wanted to finish. It would be so nice to just pass out right now. But that would be close to suicide. He knew that he was cold. He could feel it even through the numbness of exhaustion. He didn't know the altitude of this place and therefore he didn't know how long it would be before the sun came up to warm his body. He might die from hypothermia in the middle of the night. It wasn't an impossibility. That was enough for him to keep working.

Shaking himself to throw off his fatigue he picked up another dry stick that was mostly straight. With his knife, he removed the outer bark till the end was nothing but smooth wood. He sheathed his knife and picked up the bow he had made. Bending the stick even more to create slack in the fabric he wrapped the denim around the straight stick he had just finished working. Placing the stick face down in the depression of the log he had cut and placing a small amount of tinder around the vertical stick he began working the bow back and forth. As he moved the bow in a sawing motion, the denim wrapped around the vertical stick and spun the stick around. He pressed down on the stick to keep it vertical and create friction. He moved the bow back and forth as the heat between the two pieces of wood and the pile of tinder rose.

It was dark at this point, and he didn't see any smoke rise from his labor, but he did start to see a small red glow. He took away the bow and stick and gently blew into the tinder. The glow grew and with a final puff of air, a small flame leapt up. His spirits leapt with the flame, and he added more kindling to the infant fire. The flame licked and consumed the fuel with no trouble, and he added more wood till he had a good-sized fire burning.

He took stock of his wood pile; he had enough for the night. As the flame danced in front of him, he moved a little farther away and put his legs out toward the heat. The fire warmed his feet, and he was no longer afraid of losing any appendages. The fire produced a good amount of heat which surprised him. He hadn't really expected a fire of this size to do that, but it did and he wasn't complaining. He lay down on the ground next to the fire and closed his eyes. He was so tired he allowed his body to relax in front of the warm glow and he fell asleep almost instantly.

5

Meanwhile, at that same time, a few hundred miles to the south west, in the city of Los Angeles, Kenneth Pacifico, the vampire, was making his way to the state level trooper headquarters.

He was in a pretty good mood. The last report he had gotten from the chase in the mountains was that they had the young man in their sights and the helicopter was in pursuit. No one could outrun a helicopter, and the kid was probably half starved and scared shitless anyway. He probably ran straight to his agents without a second thought, begging to be brought back home.

Tracking and finding young William Setford had been more trouble than it should have been. Kenneth's own vampire House, House Dukart, had discovered how to track werewolves before they were reborn as Shape shifters. This made them easier to find, and much easier to kill.

Werewolves had been a thorn in the side of every vampire, almost since the dawn of time. Something about saving humanity from the vices and blight that vampires represented on civilization or some other such moral crusading crap. Werewolves had proven to be a threat. Vampires had wanted to live and let live, they had a right to preserve their race just as any other organism on this planet. Werewolves however, continued to interfere with their business. So, vampires had taken it upon themselves to kill every werewolf they came across.

He had tracked young William to his parents' residence outside of Modesto. His parents, weak minded, pathetic humans that they were, gave up all the information they had on William's whereabouts easily. Which is to say, they knew nothing at all.

It took months of concentrated effort to track that young monster out into the forest where they finally caught up to him. It had been a long painstaking process. But still, it would lead to one more werewolf death, and that alone was worth almost any price.

Kenneth walked in through the front doors of the State Trooper headquarters building and towards the back offices. No one stopped him, and no one questioned him. This was normal and he had access to anything and everything he needed. He made his way to a spacious office in the back, opened the door without knocking, and walked in.

There was a rather exhausted and harried looking officer sitting behind a large desk. The officer's first name was Mark; the only name Kenneth had ever used. Mark used to be in very good shape, but the stress of his job had taken its toll on his body. Kenneth's eyes could see where some of his muscle mass had deflated over the past few years and left behind only saggy skin. His arms were still a good size, but where once bulging veins ran along his arms, there was only soft skin. It was like looking at a shadow trying to fill clothes. The man presented himself as if he still had the mass he once boasted, but his clothes hung off him at odd angles. He had lost no small amount of weight.

He had folders, various loose papers, and a computer screen in front of him on his cluttered desk. He was almost shouting into the land line phone that was pressed between his ear and shoulder as he was furiously typing something on his screen, "I don't give a crap what he says! I want that helicopter in the air within the next hour and back out there! I have full authorization for this and if he has a problem with it, tell him to talk to my boss. I want that kid found and in my cells before tomorrow morning, got that!" And with that he slammed the phone back down into its receiver cradle.

Kenneth looked at Mark as the officer ran his hands through his disheveled hair. Kenneth was no longer smiling. "What happened out there, Mark? And why is this William Setford not in custody?" Kenneth stared hard at the officer as he sat down across from him.

Mark shook his head, "I don't know. The helicopter had him in their flood lights. In their goddamned flood lights! Somehow the kid was able to get away and hide in the forest. His trail wasn't picked up by the dogs till earlier this morning and by then, the trail was hours old. The kid's smart and he doesn't want to be found or picked up, that much at least we can say is fact."

Kenneth steepled his fingers in front of his face as he closed his eyes and heaved a heavy breath. He opened his eyes and lowered his hands from his face, holding Mark's gaze he barred his lips and allowed the man to see his elongated canines, the signature tell-tale sign of Kenneth's true nature and identity.

"I don't have to remind you that it was because of me

and my kind that you are currently sitting behind that desk, do I?" Kenneth asked.

Mark went pale as he shook his head, "No, no of course not Mr. Pacifico. I know who and what you are and I know who you represent. There's no need for threats."

Kenneth nodded, "This isn't a threat, just a friendly reminder. I want that boy found. I have spent considerable time and resources to find him. Time and resources that I don't appreciate being wasted by your people's incompetence to lose him again."

Mark nodded, "yes, of course we are still searching and you heard the phone call. We'll get him. I'm not going to have some freakish monster out there terrorizing and killing innocent people. No way in hell am I allowing that guy to keep on killing."

"Good," Kenneth sat back in his chair, satisfied for the moment. "Did you find anything else out there?"

Mark nodded, "We took a lot of contraband, and personal effects from, what we assume was his shelter. There was also a lot of evidence that some of our dogs and trackers found of wolves being out there. Can you believe that? Wolves in California? That's crazy right?"

Kenneth's features darkened noticeably, "Wolves? You're sure?"

"Yeah, I mean we're pretty sure. We didn't see any actual wolves, but with what the dogs smelled and what the hunters said, I can only assume they're there."

"I want them dead, all of them," Kenneth said definitively. "I don't want those killers in my state or anywhere near my home. I want them dead, and bring me the pelts. I'll pay three thousand for each wolf pelt, let your hunters know that."

Mark looked a bit shocked, "Three thousand, for each...

pelt. Are we back in the 1800's or something? Wolf bounties? Really?" Mark asked, a bit wide eyed.

"I don't find any of this funny, and you know that I take public health and safety deadly seriously," Kenneth responded.

This got the appropriate reaction from Mark and the man nodded silently as he started typing on his computer.

Kenneth stood up from his chair and turned to open the door, before stopping and looking back at the officer. "I want William found and brought to me, alive, if possible, dead is just as good. And I wasn't kidding about those wolves. I want them dead, all of them." With that Kenneth strode out of the office, closing the door firmly behind him.

6

The light grew and penetrated William's eyelids. He didn't want to wake up, so he rolled over to shield himself from the intruding light. His body groaned as he moved it, and he was perfectly happy to sleep for another two or three hours. He was only stalling the inevitable. He could never go back to sleep once he was awake. Whether his eyes were open or not, he was awake.

He opened his eyes and looked right in the face of a wolf. He jerked up with a half gasp half shout and pulled his knife free of its sheath. He overbalanced as he pulled his knife free and fell backward. As his mind caught up with him, he realized what wolf this was. The she-wolf had come back, and he sighed, exasperated at himself for being startled like that. The wolf seemed to look at him with mirth in her eyes, but he was just imagining things. He was embarrassed at himself for being so easily startled. He sheathed his blade and rolled away from the bed of coals that still smoldered next to him.

The she-wolf had brought him a present. At her feet in the early morning gloom, he saw two dead rabbits. In her jaws was that stupid piece of denim that she didn't seem to want to part with. He added some wood to the bed of coals and blew until the wood caught and became a nice fire once again. He took his blade in his hand and skinned and cleaned the rabbits as best he could. He impaled them on a stick that was just thick enough for the purpose and jamming one end into the soft ground he pulled the dead animals over the flames.

The wolf watched all of this with rapt attention. He ignored her for the most part but when he was done and there was nothing to do but allow the fire to cook the animals, he took the time to really look at his guide.

"You can drop that piece of my shorts." He had wanted to tell her that for a long time and looking her in the eyes he continued. "I have followed you this far, haven't I?" The wolf stared at him. He didn't really expect her to acknowledge him in any way and he exhaled. "I guess you're not a magical wolf."

He smiled as his mind brought up all manner of references in which magical creatures lived and talked, *Little Red Riding Hood* and *The Chronicles of Narnia*. But this was reality and yet he was following a wolf, a natural predator, to wherever she chose to lead him. He began to laugh out loud. The wolf cocked her head to the side at the sudden loud noise. He couldn't help it. He was struck by the sheer ridiculousness of his situation. This wolf had hunted and killed for him, she had led him away from danger and pursuit, at least so far. Was he just a character in some fantasy story? He laughed harder till his sides hurt and he had to roll onto his side.

"You'll probably eat me once we get to where we are going." He managed to say through his laughter. "Are you taking me to some evil wizard in the forest who wants to change me into some kind of killing monster to avenge himself upon everybody who ever doubted him?" The wolf stood there perplexed at what was happening. He hadn't laughed this hard in a long time and he found it hard to stop.

He pushed himself up into a sitting position. He wiped the tears from his eyes, and he barked out a few more laughs till he was sure that he was ok and could keep control of himself. It really was funny though. A magical wolf! Had he lost his mind?

The she-wolf stood there watching this strange behavior. She didn't move and he wondered how he looked to her right now. She did not get the joke and he wondered if wolves found anything to be humorous. Did wolves have a sense of humor? As he thought about the question he reached over and pulled one of the rabbit spits out of the ground and tossed it toward the wolf.

"You probably prefer yours rare."

The she-wolf sniffed at the dead animal and dropping the piece of denim from her mouth she began to eat the thing. He watched her tear into the flesh that she herself had caught. As she ripped deeper into her meal, he couldn't quite place it but there was something about this wolf. She had helped him last night when his strength had all but given out. She had helped him escape his valley, and she had caught him the meal which was cooking happily over the small fire he had built. She hadn't seemed afraid of the flames either.

He shook his head and grabbed the other rabbit from the fire and began to eat. The flesh of the animal was tough and singed but good and as he ate, he felt strength flow back into his body. It's amazing what a night's rest and some hot food could do for the human body. He continued to eat in silence with his four-legged companion.

The morning gloom had lifted, and the sun now shone upon them as they ate. The wolf had finished her rabbit and picking up the piece of denim, sat on her haunches waiting for him to finish. There was a good amount of meat to be had from the rabbits, but it was soon gone, and he began to clean up their campsite. Even here, a day's travel from his valley, he knew that leaving any trace of his passing would eventually bring his pursuers to him.

He cleared the campsite of all traces of them being there. When he was finished, he looked over the clearing and was satisfied that after a day, and maybe some rain, this place would look as undisturbed as the virgin snowfall of winter.

He looked at his guide and motioned to her. "Let's go." He paused for a moment and looked into the wolf's eyes. "You wouldn't happen to want to tell me where we're going, would you?"

The wolf stood up and trotted past him into the forest, not making a sound. He shook his head and whispered to himself, "I didn't think so."

7

The sun's rays were not as hot as they were yesterday. The two travelers were moving at a good pace, but he was still cool. He lost track of time as the two ate up the distances they were traveling. He felt the cool mountain air flow through his lungs and body bringing life and circulation. The sun continued up its track and reached its zenith without his notice. His eyes were rhythmically shifting from the ground to the she-wolf's tail and back again. They were not traveling in a nice crevice today. The rocky ground was open and that was enough to motivate him. They were too open out here on the rocks. There was no cover and no escape route. If they were spotted out here, they were as good as dead.

The wolf seemed to understand this as well because her pace had been increasing throughout the morning and now, they were at a run. Not a full-out sprint but more like a marathon's pace. He breathed as he concentrated on his feet and controlled his body, to not use too much energy and to stay calm and steady. He focused on his breathing, deep and even. His legs pumped thick blood throughout his body. He was in good shape but that gave him little comfort when he contemplated the vast distance they had to travel.

The wolf ran over the rock surface and didn't slow or waver in her direction, north. His mind worked on that for a moment. Could she really be taking him the couple hundred miles to Canada? He wavered in his pace as the distance that would have to be traveled on foot hit him with crushing force. That was impossible. Canada couldn't be reached by foot. You needed a car or something. A plane would be nice. He stumbled to a stop and rested his hands on his knees, breathing raggedly. *She's crazy.* If Canada was their destination, and he couldn't think of anything between where they were and that frigid northland, it would take them months to get there. He looked up. The wolf had stopped and was looking at him.

He began to hate this animal. This silent guide that had led him to the middle of nowhere and now what? She expected him to just follow her for weeks on end till they got wherever they were going? He stood up and walked toward the wolf, but he made no attempt to hide the anger and contempt from his stare. The wolf stood there watching him approach, not moving.

He growled low in his throat. "Where are we going? Are we going to Canada?" The wolf stood there staring at him. "You expect me to just follow you till God knows when, till we get to wherever you're taking me, don't you?" His muscles tensed and strained more and more with each word as he allowed his anger to build. "How in the hell do you expect us to reach Canada on foot?" His neck muscles were working, and the wolf still just stood there. "Answer me. How do you expect us to get to Canada with winter coming? Snow's going to start falling soon, especially if we keep going north the way we are."

The wolf watched and listened as he continued to raise his voice, forcing it to echo off the barren rock.

"I'm not like you," he explained. "I don't have a nice fur coat to keep me warm out here. All I have is this half vest which I wear during the *summer*." He waved his hands to take in and illustrate the barren rocks they were on. "Granted, if those fucking cops hadn't shown up and sacked my burrow and probably stolen all my gear, I wouldn't have had to leave and I wouldn't be out here with you." He jabbed a finger at the wolf and turning around he began to pace, throwing his hands around like a madman as he continued to rant, half to himself and half to his guide. His anger was building, a sensation he had not felt in a long time and the fire of it warmed his body and enflamed his purpose, giving him strength.

"What the hell do those cops want with me anyway?" He looked up at the old man in the sky, squinting from his bright glare. "What the hell is so special about me? Why couldn't they just leave me alone and let me live my life the way I wanted to live it?" He punched his hand down into his fur vest and ripped out the plastic bag that carried his life savings. All he was worth monetarily was in that bag. "Oh no, we can't have some guy out there that doesn't want the latest electronic gadget. Nope, can't have that. Everybody has to be the same and those that aren't, need to be reeducated to learn how to be like everybody else. You need a job. You need to buy shit to fill up your house or crappy apartment." He was yelling at nobody in particular, pacing and turning around, wandering in no special direction.

The she-wolf watched and listened to him sitting down on her haunches. The rock had been warmed by the sun. The piece of denim still held securely in her jaws.

He held the bag up so the wolf could see the green paper

inside. "You see this?" The wolf looked at him, her white starburst on her chest showing underneath the piece of blue denim hanging from her mouth. "This *paper* is the only thing that matters, and this is what a person's worth is measured by." The wolf continued to watch him, her golden eyes tracking his every movement. Hers was not the blank look of a dog but of an intelligent creature that was absorbing and observing everything around her.

"You see? You need a job. A crappy job you hate so you can earn more of this," He held the bag up to the sky. "You need to earn more so you can give it away again. You work your whole life to get it then spend it faster than you make it. And then you have to pay more money because you made the money in the first place. You have to pay your taxes and if you don't? We'll hunt you down." With a last frustrated growl, he threw the baggie down on the ground. A wet slapping sound met their ears. He took a few deep breaths and put his hands on his hips. The wolf continued to watch him with the same intensity as she had been all along.

They're out there, right now hunting me. The thought of being captured like some criminal and being forced to go back to that world of pettiness and greed made him want to hit something. He looked at the baggie at his feet and looked at the wolf that hadn't moved throughout his tirade. He sighed and scooped up the baggie. He jammed it back into his vest and brushing his hair roughly with his other hand he walked toward his guide. "I'm not a criminal and I won't let them catch me out here like a dog either." He hunched down low in front of his wolf companion. He looked into her golden eyes and in a much softer voice he said, "I'm sorry. I know that was unhelpful and a waste of time. I've followed you this far and I will continue to follow you, even if you are taking me hundreds of miles from here."

He stood up as a wry smile crept across his face. "I've always wanted to see Canada. I hear it's gorgeous this time of year. But we won't get there for a couple of months." He put both his hands up in front of him motioning the wolf. "After you, my lady."

The wolf kicked herself off the rock from which she was sitting and in a full run flew past him. He ran after her as they continued their trek over the barren landscape. The wolf did not keep her sprinting pace and soon she was jogging over the rocks. He fell back into his marathoner's pace keeping a good distance between himself and his wolf companion.

The sun was already on its way down from its zenith and it sat just off his left shoulder. The sun was warm but not too warm and he was comfortable. His body was sweating and the cool air around him felt wonderful.

The wolf continued on her steady course north. He couldn't see anything that might be construed as anything special about this area. All the rocks looked the same and the ground was rounded having been shaped by wind and rain. As he ran, he thought about how useless his earlier anger had been. *I was being stupid and petulant, like a child complaining, 'Are we there yet?'* Still, he hadn't really felt anger like that in a long time except two nights ago when his home had been invaded. There was strength to be had from his anger. He remembered that being the only good thing about it though. Anger is such a base primal emotion. Whereas he had learned to live with joy and happiness, the sudden rush of hatred and anger that had invaded his soul briefly seemed alien and hostile. He didn't like it and he hoped to guard against his anger in the future.

They continued to run. His pace was steadily slowing, and the wolf was matching his pace step for step. The energy that his breakfast rabbit had given him was long gone and his stomach protested at being expected to work without being fed.

The old man in the sky was being drawn nearer to the horizon and he knew that soon the ocean would claim him once again. They would need shelter for the night. But the wolf continued to run. The ground was still warm from the sun's rays as he chased after his guide with the stubborn determination of a younger sibling. *If she's not going to stop, neither am I.*

As his eyes shifted from the ground to his guide and back to the ground again, his breathing became ragged. His vision blurred, and his legs scraped against themselves. The sudden friction caused him to stumble, and he let his body collapse onto the ground. He rolled and came to a stop with his back on the warm stone. He leaned his head against the ground and looked up at the sun. The long shadows of twilight surrounded them. He watched as the sun sank ever deeper below the horizon.

How many times had he watched the sun sink into the ocean? How many times had he watched it before he came out here? Even though he had lived out here for less than two years he was certain he had watched the sun set at least twice as many times as he had throughout the rest of his life in the civilized world. This is what life should be about. Living and surviving through your own sweat, and the strength of your back, enjoying the beautiful spectacles of nature. No movie could ever hope to duplicate the sheer awesome and beautiful sight of a simple sunset. He closed his eyes and smiled as a breeze blew over his warm body drying the sweat from his face and chest.

He felt a soft, rough, and moist texture push against his shoulder. He could smell the deep musky smell of animal fur and he knew that his guide had come to check on him. He opened his eyes to find the she-wolf standing over him, prodding him with her nose, nuzzling his shoulder. He reached up around her neck and scratched at her head. He started as he realized what he was doing.

He pulled his arm down from around her neck and heaved himself up into a sitting position. The sun was touching the horizon and soon it would be pulled down under the earth. He stood up and examined his body. He had sustained a few scrapes and a bruise on his elbow but there was no blood anywhere. He took a few steps and his legs worked without protest. He looked down at the she-wolf as she stood next to him.

"We need to find a place to camp."

The wolf watched him, making no move to agree or protest with his suggestion.

He looked up and scanned his surroundings. There would be light left for about thirty to forty minutes. After that, they would need to rely on the moon and starlight which wouldn't be a problem out here on the rocks. He was sure that he wasn't going to eat tonight, and he hardened himself to that realization. What was important now was that they find someplace out of the wind. Without food, conserving body warmth was essential. After the rocks cooled, he knew they would suck every last ounce of warmth from their bodies if they had to sleep on the bare rock.

As he scanned the horizon for someplace to sleep, the wolf took off at a run. "Hey, wait," was the only thing he could gasp out before he was chasing after her. She was in a dead-out run and he was not going to keep up with her. She was running south now for some reason. She must have slowed down because he was able to just keep her in sight.

The pace was brutal, and he knew that his body would not be able to hold out much longer.

The rocks began to slope downward, and he found it a lot easier to keep up, even though he was still pushing his body to his physical limit. The wolf bounded from rock to rock over the terrain. The wolf followed a fold in the rocks and began to travel down the middle of a crease that soon widened into a crevice. But the ground was still solid rock without even a thin layer of dirt to protect their body heat. The wolf continued to run along the crevice. The crevice deepened and widened. He was running without almost any light at this point and for a moment he thought his eyes had failed him entirely. In front of him was a massive blackness that had no borders.

He stumbled to a stop, as he could just make out the pure white starburst of his guide sitting next to the black maw, waiting for him. As his eyes adjusted to the onset of night, the moonlight illuminated his surroundings. He became aware that the black maw was in fact a cave. Its black mouth was open but there was no sense of dread or danger emanating from it. He felt a comforting presence here. He walked up to his companion and reached down to scratch at her ears. The wolf growled low in her throat, and he jerked his hand away.

He entered the cave.

His feet immediately felt a soft carpet-like substance underneath him. He squatted down and felt the surface with his hand. It was moss, soft and lush. It might spread throughout the entire cave's surface. He walked deeper inside the cave. It was pitch black and he had to hold his hands out in front of himself to avoid hitting anything. After he took a dozen steps or so he felt a solid rock wall meet his outstretched hands. He smiled and breathed a sigh. The cave was tall but not very deep and that meant that no sleeping animals would sneak up on him from behind and eat him while he slept.

He smiled at his own unfounded fears and walked back toward the star-filled curtain that covered the cave entrance. Looking down at his companion he smiled. "Thank you, my lady. This will be perfect." The wolf sat there watching him, neither acknowledging nor ignoring his words. "I will definitely miss dinner but that can't be helped, can it?"

He sat down on the soft moss-covered floor and looked at the stars and his Lunar Mother, who had shrunk since last night. She was only a little more than half of her true brilliance. Soon she would disappear almost entirely and be reborn anew.

He laid back and looked straight up into the blackness that was the cave ceiling. Had anyone else lay here like he was doing right now? Had there ever been a creature or two that had called this cave home? He let these thoughts drift through his mind freely neither ignoring them nor heavily contemplating them. The day's exertion had taken its toll and as he let his body relax, his eyes closed on their own and he was asleep.

His eyes shot open, and he gasped in fear. He sat upright in his cave and desperately tried to make his mind work. He had been dreaming. He was drenched in a cold sweat. His limbs were still intact. He wiped his face with his hands as he took a few deep breaths trying to calm down.

He was sitting on the moss-covered floor of the cave that the she-wolf had led him to. He folded his arms around his bent knees. He breathed deeply, trying to make his heart slow down. He had been dreaming but he couldn't remember what had scared him so badly. All he could remember was that the dream had had something to do with wolves. His pack maybe? He couldn't be sure. In the dream, something terrible had happened or was going to happen before he woke up.

He hadn't had a nightmare in a long time, since he started living out in his forest, and the fear that still gripped him was something he hadn't known for a long time. When he was able, he stood up and walked outside the cave. His eyes had adjusted to the darkness of night, and he saw his companion was gone. *She's probably out hunting.* Still, it would have been nice to have her there. Having her there was a comfort and right now he could use a little comforting. The fear still gripped him, not for himself but for those he had left behind.

My pack.

The dream had called up some very nasty things and he couldn't help but feel more than just a little worried about his pack. Technically, he was their alpha and they wouldn't do anything without him. But these were also wild animals and if he wasn't there to lead them surely their prime beta, the old grey, would lead them. The species had lived on this planet longer than humans had and they had survived. Surely, they could survive the momentary invasion of some cops and federal agents, couldn't they?

He rested his hand on the outside wall of the cave looking at the river of dense lights in the sky. A hundred million single stars painted a band that ran through the center of the night sky, and he was comforted by their steady presence. They had always been there, watching him and watching over his pack. *The grey will watch over them and keep them safe. He did it before I came along, and he'll do it again.* Wolves knew their duty to each other, and the rest of his pack would look to the old grey for guidance till he could return, if he could return.

He slapped his open palm against the solid rock of the cave wall in frustration and regret. The force of it caused a jolt of hot pain to surge up his arm till it dissipated at his elbow. Grimacing with the sudden pain he shook out his hand muttering, "Rock beats hand." He turned away from the brilliant star field in the night sky and sat back down on the moss-covered floor.

The she-wolf would be back soon, and they would continue on at first light. He laid back and rested his head on his arm. He looked at the black ceiling as shadows danced before his eyes. He slowed his breathing and forcibly relaxed his body. He might as well get as much sleep as he could, tomorrow was going to be another rough day. With a little more difficulty than expected his eyes finally began to weigh down. He breathed and he managed to fall into a light sleep.

His shoulder was being nudged and he opened his eyes to find the she-wolf had come back. She was obviously trying to tell him it was time to get up. She was incessantly grinding her nose into his shoulder.

"All right, all right. I'm up. I'm up."

He couldn't be sure what time it was. The sun hadn't risen yet and the world was still blanketed in darkness. He pushed himself up into a sitting position and stood up. The wolf had walked outside the cave and was looking out over the star-filled sky. He walked outside the cave and the wolf started trotting along the crevice that had led them here.

He followed but sleep was still heavy in his limbs. "Can we at least walk for a bit?" The she-wolf stopped and looked back at him, the piece of denim shorts still in her mouth. The look she gave him was somewhere between, 'Don't be ridiculous' and 'What? You can't keep up?' Well, he wasn't about to let some four-legged, she-beast slave driver get the better of him, so he took a deep breath and forced his legs to move into a trot.

The wolf led him out into the crevice and picked her way along the crevice ridge. He followed suit. The light was all but nonexistent and he didn't want to hurt himself in the dark. The stars were fading, and the sky was a deep black. Dawn was approaching, he could see the purple horizon off to the east.

Even though the dawn was coming it wasn't a good idea to let the she-wolf get too far ahead of him. The wolf seemed to know exactly what speed he was capable of holding. She stayed at a threatening distance from him. If he slowed down, he would lose her in the predawn darkness. She kept him moving at a pace that he had to exert himself to maintain, but it could be done.

He was surprised to find that after a few hundred yards his legs started pumping in perfect rhythm with the wolf. Even though his stomach was protesting the exertion and not at all happy at not having been fed yesterday, he was still able to keep his body moving.

He stumbled on a lip in the rock. He swung his arms outward to regain his balance and a few steps later he was back in rhythm with the she-wolf. The sky was brightening with each passing minute, and he knew the sun would soon peak over the lip of the horizon, bathing him, his guide, and the mountains with sunlight.

He forced himself to keep pace with the wolf. They were running north and as he looked to his right, sunlight blazed forth, driving the shadows into retreat as they ran. He was almost instantly warmed by the bright light of morning. He closed his eyes and let the sun glare into his face. He found himself laughing at the warm rays of the new day. He opened his eyes not knowing where he was running with his eyes closed. He found he had veered off course and turned back to follow in the wolf's footsteps once more. He looked back north in the direction they were running and, in the distance, seeming to float above the earth, were snowcapped mountain peaks.

He knew he would not be able to survive the snow with only the clothes and equipment he had with him. A half pair of jean shorts stuffed in his pants, his long knife, a vest, and pants were not proper snow gear by any stretch of the imagination.

As he studied the snow-covered peaks in the distance the wolf turned to the west and started to descend a gentle slope. He followed and let his strides elongate to pick up speed while using less energy. His body was thankful for the rest, and he breathed at the easing of the run for however long the slight respite lasted.

As he ran down the slope of rock, he watched his wolf companion glide over the mountain. She was graceful and strong. Her tail shifted behind her, maintaining her balance. He watched as her muscles worked under her coat of black fur. She was an amazing animal.

He looked down to see where they were running to. The tree line was a sharp contrast to the barren rock they had been running on for these past few days. The pine trees here were brown. The lower half of most of the trees were dry and looked all but dead. That wasn't a good sign if they were hoping to find water and he was thirsty, come to think of it. The trees were spaced apart from each other and offered very little protection from the elements or prying eyes.

As they passed through the outer line of trees and deeper into this particular part of the mountains, he was relieved to see that only those outermost trees were dying. Here, inside this part of the forest, the trees were spaced closer together and they were green. He was surrounded by strong tall woodlands that would have made a nice refuge. But he knew that they were not staying here, at least not for very long.

They ran east going deeper into the woods. The sunlight had very little power. The canopy above and around them was more than enough to block the sun's rays. Here, in the shade of the forest, they ran upon the pine-needle-strewn forest floor. He watched as his guide darted and jumped in between the trees. He had a little trouble following her, but they were on a small trail, so he knew where they were going if he lost sight of her a moment or three.

His feet were cushioned by the dirt and the pine needles of the forest floor. Again, he was surprised to find that he was keeping so strong a stride in his running. He should be close to passing out with exhaustion and hunger. His stomach was making itself known to him, but he found that he could ignore the grumbling, and his body was responding well, almost too well.

They continued running east and the trees grew denser around them. The trunks began to hug closer to each other, and the shadows of the morning grew darker. The trail they were following all but disappeared, and he was having difficulty maintaining his pace as more of his attention was being forced to concentrate on not running into a tree and avoiding bushes, branches, and stray rocks that had found their way into his path.

They continued to run on for a long while. His stomach, not liking being ignored, was making louder and louder noises and he was beginning to feel lightheaded. Nothing serious, he was sure that he was not going to pass out, but the sensation could not be shaken away either. That feeling persisted.

Farther east they traveled. Eventually, they came to a small lake or more of a large pond. The sun was reflected off its perfect blue surface. The surrounding trees and rocks framed the place beautifully. *Pretty as a postcard and twice as dangerous.* Water was the sign of civilization. And what better place for cops to look for someone than by bodies of water? He had been running for a few days and nights now, but cops had that helicopter and other vehicles. They could be watching this lake right now just waiting for him to show himself.

He crouched down next to his guide, who was staring out over the water. He was at her eye level and together they scanned the tree line. The she-wolf raised her nose to the air and sniffed, tasting the wind currents that blew off the water's surface. He couldn't see any disturbance at all. No shifted dirt, no bent or broken branches, no movement at all, except for the slight ripples that played out across the lake from the wind, sending shimmering sunlight dancing on the lake's surface.

His guide must have been satisfied as well because she walked down to the lake and, dropping the piece of denim from her mouth, began to drink. Following close behind, he lay down next to the wolf and drank the frigid water. As the cold liquid flowed down his hot throat, he was chilled and had to grip his neck to try to warm it up again. He gasped and sputtered as the frigid temperature of the water found its way painfully into his stomach. He could almost hear the water splash down into his empty gut.

The she-wolf continued to lap up water from the lake. As he lowered himself back down to the lake, he took smaller sips. The frigid water was definitely easier to handle in smaller doses. The water chilled him to the core and even though he had been running all morning, even the heat of the rising sun was not able to keep him warm. That was good because he knew he was not going to get to rest anytime soon, they still had such a long way to go.

Having satisfied their thirst, the she-wolf turned away and began walking around toward the southern side of the lake. This did not go unnoticed. They had run or trotted everywhere since they left his valley and now, they were walking. He wasn't upset at this new slower pace, but his mind began to think something was wrong. The wolf seemed ok. She wasn't walking with a limp and there was no visible injury. If anything, the cool lake water had rejuvenated both him and her. She was walking with more of a spring in her step and she was almost bouncing over the terrain. But they walked. He hadn't argued with her so far and he was not about to start now. Besides his stomach would not be satisfied with only water for very long, and he knew that even though he felt ok he couldn't keep running without food.

They made their way cautiously around to the south side of the lake staying deep within the shadows of the trees. They had to walk around various boulders and underbrush. They had to climb up steep inclines instead of risking straying too close to the water. Even walking he was soon sweating again with this different kind of exertion. *No wonder we're walking.* The lake wasn't very big, but the sun was already high in the sky by the time they reached the southern side of it.

Here there was a nice clearing. Better stated, it was a less densely populated area of trees. The sun filtered through here nicely and he was reminded of those manicured campgrounds that he had often camped at with his family so long ago. He mentally pointed out where the cast iron grill would have gone. Over to his right should have been a concrete slab for RVs and the connecting outlets of power, water, and sewage. Tents would have been scattered around in domes of bright green and orange. There would have been a heavy wooden camping table next to the grill. And the bathrooms would have been off somewhere with a wide gravel road leading to it from the campsite. He found himself sneering at the mental imagery. People 'camped' to 'get away from it all.' What they were really doing was telling themselves that they were 'roughing' it and that they were still men with ties to their ancestors who had to live that way because they didn't have air-conditioned apartments and two-story homes to live in a few hundred years ago.

He wiped the mental image from his mind. The wolf had gone to lay down in the shade of a tree. She had dropped the piece of denim from her mouth and was half lying on it, as she rested her head on her folded forelegs. As he walked over to her, she lifted her golden eyes watching him approach. He sat down and rested his back against the large tree trunk, letting his eyes close. He couldn't feel the wind anymore, but the shade of the tree was enough to keep him cool and safe from the sunlight. He rested his arms down at his sides and felt the soft dirt and pine needles that he was now sitting on. He smiled at the feel of the earth. Moss-covered rock was soft enough, but it wasn't earth, and he was glad to be off rock for the time being.

He opened his eyes and looked over at his guide. Her eyes were closed, and she was breathing evenly. She had fallen asleep. That was ok. He was sure she had gotten less rest in the past few days than he had. He gently raised himself up from his spot on the ground, careful to not make any sound or disturbance so as not to wake his sleeping companion. He tiptoed away from the sleeping wolf and went off into the forest.

He had to get something to eat. He walked off toward the lake again and started hunting for fruit-bearing bushes or roots, anything that was edible and wouldn't make him puke. He was pretty sure he couldn't afford to puke up anything right now. Nor could he afford to get sick at all. He looked for the signs that would tell him of food. He eventually found some wild berries and a small patch of miner's lettuce. He gathered the lettuce and picked one berry from the bush, rubbing the juices of the berry on his arm. He couldn't identify the berries and he had to check to see if the berry was toxic. He scratched where the berry juice was wiped on his skin to see whether he was allergic to it or not.

As he waited for his body to respond to the test, he munched on some of the miner's lettuce and looked around at the mountain around him. It really was peaceful here. The wind had picked up since they first came here, and he felt a chill run through him. He turned his gaze up to the sky and frowned. The perfect blue of the morning sky was now being invaded by a thick front of clouds that was sweeping in from the west. The clouds were a light grey on the fringes of the front. Deeper inside the clouds turned an ugly dark grey to almost black. The clouds promised rain and not just a light autumn shower either.

He had some time but not much. He looked down at the berry juice on his arm. He wiped the juice away with his hand and studied his arm. There was no redness or irritation which was a good sign. He took another berry and squeezed some of its juice on his lips, letting the juice sit.

He didn't feel anything, but he let the juice sit for several minutes. He searched for more patches of miner's lettuce and other berries. If the berries tested ok then he would need more, especially if they were forced to stay here because of the storm. He found another patch of lettuce and he gathered the vegetation. He decided that it had been enough time for the berry juice test and licked his lips clean.

The berries had a rich flavor that spoke of summer, the way that fresh blackberries right off the vine taste like summer. There was no trace of any harmful tangy sensation. He decided that the berries were ok, but he wasn't taking any chances out here in the wilderness. He gathered a good number of them, but he decided not to eat them for at least another hour or so. If something were harmful about these berries, he would know about it by then. Gathering as much miner's lettuce and berries as he could carry, he rushed back to where the she-wolf was sleeping.

The sky had already started to dim, and the wind was picking up. He placed the food on the ground near her and began searching for fallen logs and large branches. He could make a lean-to with little problem if he could find the materials for it. The sky was darkening by the minute, and he knew that it could start raining at any time.

He searched the area. He didn't see any sizable logs or pieces of wood at all. What he did find was a fallen tree that was resting against a small boulder on the mountainside. He dug out some earth around the boulder, clearing a floor area. Once that was done, he backed away and began to break off the lower branches of the surrounding trees, hacking them with his knife as needed. As he broke off the bigger branches from the trees, he leaned the green branches up against the fallen tree truck.

Nature never waited for anyone and as he was preparing their shelter, the sky opened up and it started raining heavily. He threw branches over the shelter trying to make it as resistant to water as possible. The rainwater soaked through his skins. He worked through the discomfort. They needed a shelter and a place to get dry. He finished the shelter in a short period of time, but he was already soaked through to the bone.

He rushed back through the forest to where his companion and food store was. She was awake and sitting under a densely branched tree, staying relatively dry. He picked up his pile of food and motioned for her to follow him. She looked at him with the piece of denim in her mouth and came out of her sheltered spot beneath the tree. He led her to the shelter he had just prepared.

They moved through the trees as the rain fell heavier by the minute. The ground was carpeted in soft pine needles but there would soon be mud and running rainwater streams everywhere. Good for them to erase any traces of their being there. Bad for them because the water was likely to go anywhere and everywhere.

They made their way to the shelter and upon seeing the dry alcove under the large tree trunk, the she-wolf bolted in front of him. She raced toward the dry piece of ground and once under the shelter she shook all the water from her fur. He dove in after her and put his food down next to the boulder. The she-wolf lay down at the other end of the shelter under the tree trunk. She wedged her body so there was very little clearance between her body and the wood. She had dropped the piece of denim from her mouth and was watching him with her head resting upon her forearms.

He turned toward the shelter opening and moved some branches around closing the entrance. It wasn't as good as his burrow had been, but for literally throwing this shelter together he was proud of himself. The wolf didn't seem to complain. She already had her eyes closed and was sleeping peacefully. He leaned his back against the boulder and began to eat his meal.

The lettuce was crunchy and crisp even with the added

water. The berries were good, and he soon finished the whole pile. He wished he had gathered more food. His stomach was not full, not by a long shot, and he knew that it would soon be growling again from hunger. But it really couldn't be helped. He raised himself as high as he could off the ground and took off his wet vest. Wiping the excess water from his clothes he put the vest back on and sat down away from the now wet spot on the ground.

He found himself very close to his wolf companion and her warmth was very inviting. He slid up to her as much as possible while maintaining some distance. He knew she didn't like to be petted, and she probably liked having her personal space invaded much less. He stayed a good five to six inches away from her, but she produced heat like a radiator. He stopped moving and listened to the rain.

His little shelter was a good one even if it was hastily made. The rain was not intruding on them, and he was able to just listen to the storm. He allowed his eyes to grow heavy. His close proximity to the warmth of the she-wolf, the dry shelter, and his belly being less empty than it had been, coupled with the last few days of heavy exertion all worked on him and he was soon asleep.

8

He was back in his valley. The full moon had risen, and he had been transformed again. He howled into the night sky, calling to his pack. There was an answering howl off in the distance and he ran toward the call. He glided over the terrain, darted in between the trees, and tore through the underbrush. He was free in ways that he could never be in his human form, freedom through movement and speed.

He rushed down the hillside, howling as he went. The responding call seemed farther off than it had been only a few moments ago. He ran toward the responding call. Any moment his pack would be with him, and they would hunt. His heart was always light when he thought about being with his pack reveling in the simple joy of the hunt and the exhilaration of the kill.

He leapt over the small river that cut his valley in two. The water gurgled and bubbled over the rocks as it had always done. He stopped on the other side of the river and called out again. Something was wrong. This time the responding call was even further away. Why wasn't his pack making their way toward him? He was their alpha and they should be coming toward him not going away. He made himself run even faster and lowered himself to all fours. He tore through the trees at breakneck speeds. Clipping the underbrush and pulling branches with him in his wake, he ran toward where the last call had emanated from.

He continued to run. He didn't really notice that he was running west toward the ocean and right then he didn't care. His mind seemed fixated on finding his pack and nothing else mattered. He called out again. His howl reverberated off the valley walls, and the response was so faint he wasn't sure he had heard it at all. He kept running. His mind was wildly thinking of every type of horrible scenario it could and even though he was running faster than he ever had before he was breaking out into a cold sweat.

He continued on in almost a complete panic. His legs were fear-driven to move faster and faster. His pack had to be ok. Where were they? He called again and as he strained his ears to hear the response, he lost sight of the ground. The ground fell away from under him and as he fell down an impossibly long almost completely black drop he looked up and saw the old grey standing on the cliff edge looking down at him.

He awoke with a scream and knocked his head against the tree roof of his shelter. The pain stifled the fear-induced yell and produced one of pain from his lips. The she-wolf raised her head in alarm with a slight whine. She almost sounded concerned.

As he rubbed his head with his dirt-covered hand he tried to hold on and remember the dream he had just had.

"It's ok. I'm ok. Sorry about that. Just go back to sleep. Everything's ok."

She watched him and instead of lying back down she

picked up the piece of denim she had been laying on, stood up, and moved to the other side of the shelter with the higher roof and stood over him.

He watched her move around him, and he twisted to face her with his hand massaging his forehead. He looked at her, still in pain from bumping his head on this stupid tree trunk and watched her as she simply stood there watching him.

"Why do I get the feeling you have been watching over me for a lot longer than I think?" he said as he took his hand away from his head. The pain from the bump he had given himself was dissipating and would soon be nothing more than a mild nuisance. He looked into her golden eyes and not for the first time he saw intelligence. There was a depth to her eyes, a sense that she understood everything that was going on around her.

He expected nothing less from a wolf. If she had been a dog he would not have seen that intelligence in her eyes. Also, she was still a wild animal and one that, while he was human, could rip him to shreds with very little trouble. "I'm harder to kill than I look."

Why did he just tell her that? She had made no motion toward him, no threatening gestures. She stood there watching him.

Outside the small shelter, the storm continued. The rain hadn't increased but it hadn't slowed either. It would be night soon and he was content to stay here where it was dry and recover his energy from his exhausted body.

He rotated around into a sitting position facing her. She also sat down on her haunches and moved back toward the boulder, giving him a little bit more room.

"Do you have a name?" The she-wolf cocked her head to

the side as if wondering why he would ask such a ridiculous question. "No, you're right. That was a stupid question."

They sat there for a time listening to the rain. The she-wolf was looking at him and though he knew that she was watching every move he made, she was also paying attention to the storm and what was going on outside of the shelter.

He felt safe around her. Even though she was a wild animal she had led him here and she had followed him when he led her to this shelter. Trust was not easily given by wild animals but two companions traveling together, protecting each other was something he hadn't ever really experienced. Sure, he had had friends back home. He was odd, but he still had a few people who respected him and he liked being around: Brian, Nate, Dave, and Corey. All those guys he hung out with, spent time with, and shared jokes with. *We were just a group of guys that hung out together.* None of them knew to the extent that he had come to hate everything the human condition encompassed, but those guys, even though they did share some of those base characteristics, weren't as bad as the disease that American humanity had become.

But out here he knew that this wolf was watching out for him and he in turn was going to watch out for her. She had run with his pack and when he was able, he would protect her just as he had his pack. Feeling very comfortable under the gaze of the she-wolf, he lay back on the soft ground and let his eyes grow heavy once more. He fell back down into a comfortable deep sleep.

His eyes opened slowly in the dark of the shelter. He could tell that it was night or at least morning was still a ways off. He lifted his head and looked around the shelter to find that his companion was gone. *Probably out hunting.* The thought of the hunt and red meat immediately made his mouth water and his stomach rumble. But he shook his head in disappointment. Even if the she-wolf were able to catch something, and he had no doubt that she could, there was nothing to light a fire with. The rain which had stopped, he now noticed, still had more than enough time to thoroughly soak every piece of wood in their vicinity. And even though he liked the taste of blood and the taste of raw meat he wasn't sure about the health risks. While he was in werewolf form the meat didn't seem to bother him. But he wasn't sure about what it would do to his human body.

The morning was closer than he thought, and the sun would soon rise over the horizon. He grabbed large handfuls of the branches that were the walls of the night's shelter and scattered them around the forest walking as far as around five hundred yards away to mask the placement of the large amount of wood.

The sun's rays found their way under the looming, dripping tree branches, and he washed his hands in the golden glow. The sun did not have much strength yet and the light didn't bring much warmth but after the gloom of yesterday, seeing the pure untainted sun rise and filter through the trees was a welcome relief.

When he was finished disassembling the shelter, he found a gently sloping rock that was almost completely dry and sat down waiting for his companion to return. He inhaled the scents of the forest. It did not smell unlike his valley but there were subtle differences. He could detect no trace of cedar pines. The air smelled more earthy here than in his valley. He supposed that was because this was more of a flat expanse and the wind was not aided by the terrain, so instead of being pushed along, like in his valley, the wind was more stagnant here. The standing lake might also have something to do with it. This small difference would make it harder to detect things by smell. Without wind, the scent would just sit in place making it harder for them to move and anticipate the movements of others around them.

He looked around himself and studied the trees and the forest. It wasn't good to just sit here. Besides he was hungry, and the she-wolf could take care of herself.

He moved through the forest, making as little noise as possible. He really did need to learn how those Native Americans did that silent walk thing. Grabbing a nearby stick, he made his way to the lake and, after scanning the shore and tree line to make sure he was alone, he drank the cold mountain water. He took the stick and dipped it into the cold lake water. He jammed it into his mouth and scrubbed his teeth. It would be better if he had some salt or baking soda but he didn't, so he had to make do with what he had. When he was finished, he rinsed his mouth out with lake water and threw the stick into the lake. He watched it splash into the gentle surface making small ripples that made their way back to the shore.

With that business taken care of, he rose off the ground and walked back into the woods a good hundred to two hundred yards away from the lake and relieved himself next to a moderately sized redwood. He began searching for more of the berries that he had yesterday and another patch of miner's lettuce.

The rain-dripping branches didn't do much to impede his progress but every few steps or so a large drop would plop down on his head or arms. He didn't have a fear of getting wet, it was the fact that even though he had lived out among nature for so long he was still very acutely aware of just how many things out here could kill him. In werewolf form, it was a different story, but in his frail human form, he was just as exposed now as he had been when he first walked into his valley.

He found a bush that was bursting with those tasty berries from yesterday and he ate many of them right then. He left a decent amount on the bush. He was careful even when eating to not leave anything that might draw attention to his passing, including how many berries off a bush he ate. *There are so many ways to track a person and very few of them have anything to do with footprints.* If those cops ever made it out this far away from his valley, he would be very impressed, but he would not allow himself to become over-confident.

With a little more searching he found another bush full of berries and was able to find a good-sized patch of miner's lettuce. He ate his fill. A few days ago, he had eaten almost a full half of a dear and was fine. Today he ate some lettuce and berries and was fine. Did changing from human to werewolf do something to his metabolism as well?

He heard movement behind him. He dove and crouched behind a nearby tree and waited. The black and white she-wolf came trotting through the underbrush and walked around the tree to face him. She was panting and she looked at him with what might be considered a smile.

His forehead creased. "What are you so happy about?"

The she-wolf turned around and trotted back the way she had come. She stopped and looked over her shoulder at him. She wanted him to follow her.

Sighing, he shook his head and looked up toward the blue morning sky, "What have you gotten yourself into now, I wonder?" This was said more to himself than to the wolf. He walked after the animal shaking his head.

The she-wolf started jogging once she saw he was

following her. She led him away from the lake and deeper into the forest. His body was responding. He had no problem keeping pace with the wolf and he kept her in sight, despite the dense underbrush that they were passing through.

It seemed that their pace was increasing at a steady rate and before long he was in a full-out run. He noticed that they were heading north once again. Why weren't they traveling along the rocky terrain that they had run on for the past few days? It didn't really matter to him except that having to run over bushes and around trees was a lot harder than running on open rock and he found himself wondering just how long he would be able to keep this up.

They raced through the forest. The she-wolf jumped and glided through the rough terrain. He let his long legs carry him over the underbrush and keep pace with the wolf using his long strides. He lost himself in the motion of the run, his legs pumping and his eyes moving back and forth between the ground and his guide.

They came upon a dense part of the forest, and they were forced to slow down. The wolf immediately turned westward, and he followed. He soon saw what it was that the wolf had seemed so happy about.

Lying on the ground next to a rather large, dead-looking pine tree was the fresh corpse of a small deer. The she-wolf trotted around to the other side of the dead animal and sat down on her haunches next to the piece of denim that she had left in the dirt.

He wished that it hadn't rained last night and that he had some dry wood. As it was, he didn't have a way to cook the animal. He looked down at the carcass. It looked good. The dead deer had claw marks down its back and a very distinctive bite mark on its neck. It was fresh and flies hadn't gathered yet, but they probably would, especially in the growing heat of the late morning. The thing had a pool of blood that was draining out of it, resting a few feet from the thing. The deer had not been eaten or disturbed in any way except that it had been killed. The she-wolf had not taken her share before she had led him here. She was going to wait and share the full kill with him. *That is very thoughtful of you, my lady.*

His body would need the protein. He wasn't going to argue that fact, but he had always been wary about eating raw meat out here in the wilderness. But he didn't want the kill to go to waste either. He succumbed to his animal instincts and decided to eat the thing raw. He wrenched his knife free from its sheath and plunged it deep into the animal's belly. With a forceful jerk, he ripped the blade up toward its throat. More blood came gushing out of the animal and his hands were covered in the red ichor.

He reached his hand up into the animal and ripped out the heart. He raised it up to the wolf. The wolf sniffed at the upheld organ. He dropped it onto the ground at her feet, being careful to not have it touch the piece of fabric that was lying there. The wolf sniffed at it once more and then lunged at it with her jaws and in one motion the organ was gone, and her mouth was red with the blood of the morsel.

He smiled at her hunger and reaching into the deer once more he pulled out the liver and placed it at her feet. The wolf sniffed it and in the same motion as before the liver also disappeared. He continued to rip out the vittles of the dead animal and one at a time he placed them at the feet of his guide. She would sniff every piece of meat first then in one smooth, vicious motion she would devour the meat without remorse or hesitation.

He began carving into the flank of the deer, shaving

away strips of the rich red flesh and eating them raw. The animal flesh satisfied him in ways that fruit and vegetation just couldn't do. He felt a slight twinge of guilt over not being able to build a fire and cook the animal properly. This meal might make him sick or kill him. He understood all these risks, but he kept eating. The meat was rich and good, and he couldn't bring himself to stop till he was full.

Once he had had his fill, he cleaned the knife on the ground and sheathed it. He then tore into the animal with his hands, mangling the carcass. He couldn't just leave the thing having been obviously carved by a man-made knife. He dug his hands into it and ripped at the flesh. The she-wolf seemed to understand what was going on as well because she tore into the thing with her teeth, mashing and eating the animal.

After the deer looked as close to being eaten by wolves as they could make it appear he stood up. He would love to go back to that lake and wash himself off. The deer's blood was already drying and very sticky. He was afraid to touch anything. He looked down and saw that his knife's handle was covered in drying deer blood and that would attract some unwanted attention.

He looked down at the wolf. "You wouldn't happen to know where a guy could get cleaned up would you?"

The wolf picked up the piece of denim once more. She looked at him as he looked around with his hands held away from his sides. The wolf turned and jumped toward the north. She landed and stopped, looking back over her shoulder at him.

He took one last look around him, holding his hands up and away from him, and shaking his head he followed his guide. She ran gracefully through the trees, and he followed her as he was careful to not touch himself or anything else with his blood-covered hands. He felt ridiculous running with his hands out in front of him. But it couldn't be helped. He had to be sure he didn't leave any traces that could be followed.

His mind reached into itself, and he found himself thinking about his pursuers. Federal agents did not just give up on finding someone. If they wanted to find you, they would find you, it was that simple. Especially since they had to know they had just missed him. It had been a close thing to be sure, but they had to know that he had been at his burrow recently. The biggest culprit that pointed to the habitation of his burrow was that half-eaten fish he had saved. Fish, even smoked, did not keep very long. That being said the sweep of his valley was probably completed by now. Once they found no one there they would expand their search. Which direction they would search was a question that he had done his best to make the answer extremely hard.

It is possible that the cops had followed him. It was possible but not likely. He hadn't heard any helicopters in pursuit of them and the wolf had not given any indication that they were being followed. She had been keeping a very grueling pace though. This troubled him. Now that he thought about it, they had been running, as they were now, for three days straight. Except for yesterday when they got some rest during the storm, and when they had stopped at night to camp along the way. She had been driving them farther and farther north at ever-increasing speeds.

The trees gave way to a wide-open meadow. The wolf skirted the edge of the meadow staying within the shade of the trees. He followed and marveled again at the intelligence of the animal that he was following. She had to know that they were not out of danger from pursuit, and she was being just as cautious as he was to avoid being detected.

They looped around the outside of the meadow, following its boundary to the east, then northeast, and north again. The she-wolf stopped and trotted away from the northern boundary of the meadow and led him to a small creek that bordered the meadow on the north side. The she-wolf immediately dunked the piece of fabric in the water and shook it under the cold creek water. Once she was satisfied, she dropped the soaked piece of fabric at her feet and lapped up the water, drinking deeply.

He fell to his knees and plunged his blood-covered hands into the water. Scrubbing them till they were no longer red, he wiped the water off on his deer skin pants. Leaning over the creek he lowered his head to drink. The water was cold and slid down his throat almost painfully, but he drank the water, thankful for the thirst-quenching liquid.

He took out his knife and cleaned the handle and the blade. The deer blood had dried but with only a little difficulty the blade came clean. He looked over at his guide and she was standing up, facing southward away from the creek. Sheathing his blade, he stood up and looked in that direction as well.

He couldn't see anything, but the rigid posture of the wolf told him that something was not right. He looked out over the meadow and saw nothing unusual. The she-wolf remained where she was. He could see all her muscles were tight and she was ready to move in an instant. He couldn't figure out what it was that was making her so wary.

He heard the faint distinctive sounds of helicopter blades. His eyes widened in shock and fear. They had eluded the cops for three or four days now, but the search had obviously caught up with them. As the realization of what was happening took precious seconds to register in his mind, the she-wolf bolted and tore off northward jumping over the creek. He broke away from where he was and ran after the wolf. The wolf moved in between the trees and stayed within the shadows. He had to jump and dodge the surrounding trees just to keep the wolf in sight.

The helicopter was getting closer by the minute. It wasn't traveling very fast, at least by its standards, but its current speed was still enough to overtake them. He continued to run after his companion. She seemed to know where she was going and he had no idea where he was, exactly. Nor did he know where they could conceal themselves from the searching eyes of the helicopter.

The wolf tore through the tall grass of the forest floor. He forced himself to run faster. Soon the tall grass gave way to pine needles once more. The sound of the helicopter was not changing at all, except that it was growing steadily louder, which meant the helicopter wasn't really searching it was traveling in a straight line. If they were looking for him, wouldn't they be moving in a search pattern? This thought gave him some comfort. This helicopter must not be looking for him. It could just be a news helicopter or a weather or traffic helicopter. It could be an airlift helicopter coming to pick up some poor hiker who had broken his legs. He breathed a little easier. This helicopter probably wasn't looking for him and he allowed himself to slow down. There couldn't be any danger because the thing wasn't searching for anything. He heaved a deep sigh of relief and slowed down to a good cross-country pace. The wolf was still darting in and out of the trees.

He was confused by her panicked speed. She was an animal after all, and she hadn't slowed down at all. He soon lost her in the underbrush of the forest as the helicopter continued to grow louder. He pulled himself to a stop. He rested his hands on his knees and looked around almost helpless. Why had the wolf just taken off like that? She had to know that he was only human, and he couldn't possibly hope to keep the full sprint pace that she was setting.

As he walked off after his guide the helicopter sound was extremely loud. The thing must be close to the ground. That couldn't be normal. All at once the fear that had gripped him at the creek flooded back into him. He had to hide. He was frozen on the spot looking for a good place to do so. His body couldn't move, it just rotated in place as his eyes tried to find what he was looking for. As he was twisting around, a large force plowed into him, lifting him off his feet, and into a nearby bush.

His instincts took over then and he reached for his knife. The black and white she-wolf was standing over him with her snout very close to his nose. She didn't look happy, and he didn't move. Her legs were straddling his body, but she was resting her weight on his chest.

He tried to look up and around her, but her body obstructed his view. Her head was pointed toward the noise of the helicopter. She was looking at it through the branches and leaves of the bush that she had pushed him into. He looked up and over the wolf's head and he saw the helicopter. It was definitely not a news or traffic helicopter. In fact, it looked like a helicopter from that movie he saw a while ago. It was called, some kind of bird down. His eyes narrowed as he studied the black helicopter in the sky. *Black Hawk Down,* that was the name of the movie. Was that a Black Hawk? From what he remembered from the movie it looked very similar. *What is a Black Hawk doing out here?*

Deep down he knew that this military helicopter could only be out here for one reason, him.

He pulled his head under the she-wolf's body as much as he could while tucking his legs up under the bush. He tried to make himself as small as possible, and not for the first time, he was grateful for his skins. They would serve to camouflage him. What could be more natural in a forest than a wolf standing guard over her kill from others that would take away her hard work?

He smiled at the animal that was standing over him. She had never let him down and she had never abandoned him either. The helicopter passed overhead without hesitation or slowing down. He stayed under the protective warmth and cover of his guide till the noisy helicopter had dissipated, signaling that it had traveled a sufficient distance north of them.

The wolf stayed very rigid and ready; every sense was straining to detect anything that might be abnormal. Once the sound of the helicopter had faded the wolf slowly removed herself from his body and let him stand up. He looked at his guide and marveled at her. She had led them into the forest yesterday morning. If they had been out on the open rock of the mountain they would have been found and he was pretty sure that neither himself nor his guide could outrun a helicopter. Had she known that this helicopter was coming? Or had she simply known that it was going to rain yesterday, and she led them to a place where they could travel and find shelter when they needed to? Not for the first time he found himself thinking that there was more to this particular wolf than he had first imagined.

She turned eastward and took off at a run. He followed her. Their pace was not a full-out sprint and even though his breathing became deep and heavy he could still make out the mechanical sounds of the helicopter off in the distance. The wolf was careful to stay close to the trees and he scraped his legs against tree bark and bushes as he attempted to directly follow her line of travel.

After some time, he couldn't hear the sound of the helicopter anymore. He knew that even though he couldn't, his guide still could, and she was pushing them faster and faster to the east back toward the open rock that they had been traveling on before they had entered this forest. *What is she thinking?* If the helicopter turned around, they would be sitting ducks out there on the open rock. It couldn't be helped though as the wolf was running in an unwavering line east.

He had trusted in her, and she had probably just saved him from capture. She did know what she was doing. She was not just a stupid instinctive animal. She was intelligent and she had kept him alive and safe so far on their journey. He had nothing else to do but shut off his overly logical mind and just follow the she-wolf. For better or for worse she was the leader and he found that he did trust her. *Imagine, a human being placing his trust in an animal.* This wasn't just any animal. She was a wolf, protector and predator. And right now, she was all he had.

They continued eastward sliding from shadow to shadow, hiding from the sight of the sun as well as the sight of anyone else who might want to be watching them. As he ran after his guide, he found that they had been increasing their speed, because he was running a lot faster now than he was this morning. It was a very liberating feeling, to move at these speeds without being tired. Running like this was true freedom. But his mind was troubled by the fact that his body was even capable of it. He was running at speeds that matched the she-wolf and from here he could see that she was exerting herself to maintain this speed. *She is working hard while I am just gliding along the ground making it look easy.*

He decided to test his speed and forced himself to move even faster. He began to catch up to his guide. Even through the underbrush and staying inside the tree shadows he was able to not only match her speed but surpass it. He became a little concerned at this new ability of his. What did this mean? He didn't know and he didn't have time to worry about the consequences of his speed. He overtook the wolf, and looking over his shoulder, he winked at her.

The wolf looked at him and seeing him wink at her she pressed her body lower to the ground and shot forward in a burst of impossible speed, even for a wolf. If this had been a cartoon a trail of fire would have lit behind her as she took off. He lowered his head and forced himself to move even faster just to keep her in his field of vision.

This was definitely not natural. The ground seemed to be moving out behind him like a treadmill and all he was doing was lifting his legs. This was the easiest running he had ever experienced and yet he found himself wondering what was causing this to happen. Was this just another side effect of him being a werewolf?

He didn't know and right now he didn't care so much about the how. Right now, the only thing he was really interested in was putting as much distance between them and that helicopter as possible.

It didn't take long before they reached the tree line, and the open expanse of flat rock met them once more. The wolf turned north and dodged in between the widened spaces between the half-dead trees and he followed. They had slowed their pace and were now, rather cautiously, running northward.

He could see the wolf rotate her head back and forth.

She was looking for or listening to anything that might warn her of danger. He couldn't help but do the same thing. He had let himself be lulled into a false sense of security over the past few days, but the sight of that helicopter reminded him that something to do with the federal government wanted him found.

Why would the government want to find me? There had to be dozens of missing persons, a lot of them much younger than he was, out there. Why would the government spend this much time and money on trying to find him?

His mind reached back to the night he was forced to leave his valley. Those guys in the hazmat suits had taken briefcases out of his burrow. At the time he thought that those briefcases held all his stuff but looking back now he wasn't so sure. If they had been from the government then they were looking for something very specific and they had known that he had been living there. Did those guys know what he was? If they did then he was in very real danger and he couldn't afford to be caught. Cops didn't use military helicopters. If those guys found him, being taken back to civilization was the least of his worries.

He looked northward and he saw the massive snow-capped mountain in the distance. It looked closer than it had yesterday, but that was probably his imagination. The wolf continued to weave her way in between the trees. The dirt gave way almost entirely to the rock of the mountain and he found that his footing was less stable. He couldn't get any kind of grip from his feet. He was forced to slow down even more.

The wolf must have caught his slowed pace when she had been looking around because she matched pace with him. They continued to move northward. The sun began his descent in the afternoon sky. His legs began to protest the constant movement and his body didn't like him very much right now either. His abdomen cramped up and he found it hard to breathe. He slowed down even more holding his side.

The wolf ran ahead for a time but again she must have seen him struggling with his body because she doubled back to run next to him. With the wolf at his side, the pain in his side seemed less of a problem. He berated himself for not being tougher and what a wimp he must be letting a little cramp slow him down as much as it was.

The wolf ran at his side for a good while. The cramp didn't let up and he was forced to run at a slower and slower pace. He reminded himself that there was a military helicopter out there looking for him. There was somebody from the government that wanted him found. He felt more than just a slight twinge of guilt over the fact that it was the she-wolf at his side that had saved him from being seen but he just couldn't make himself run any faster through the pain. The pain was not dissipating at all; in fact, it was only getting worse.

He stumbled but the pain in his side and the exhaustion that had settled over his worn body prevented him from keeping his footing and he fell hard to the ground. The wolf jumped away from him as he skidded to a halt in the shallow dirt of the tree line. His first thought was to get under some cover. When he tried to move a bolt of sharp hot pain shot up through his leg. *I've just broken my leg.* He thought with horror and panic. He immediately took control of himself and shook that thought away. He couldn't have broken his leg from falling down. He was still holding the cramp in his side. He rolled over onto his back and closing his eyes he breathed a few deep breaths. The cramp wasn't going anywhere, and the added pain of his leg wasn't making any of this any easier.

He braced himself for the pain and moved his legs. He could feel his toes and his legs did respond but the pain that shot up into his body was so intense he had to stifle a yell. *What the hell happened?* His leg wasn't broken, if it were, he wouldn't have been able to move it at all. He wiggled his toes, no pain there. Then he tried rotating his ankles. Pain erupted from his ankle. He must have twisted it. He lifted himself up into a sitting position and felt up and down his legs. There was nothing wrong with his legs and he was able to bend them slightly. As far as he could tell it was just his ankle. That was good but why was he in such pain? He felt around the injured part of his foot and leg. He couldn't feel anything protruding or abnormal. Ok, he twisted his ankle. He would have to just rest for a while till the pain went away.

His wolf guide was walking around him, she was on guard, watching and listening for anything out of the ordinary. He continued to massage his legs and hurt ankle. His left leg could move without any problem but every time he tried to move his right leg pain shot up it. He wasn't going any farther today.

He scooted along on his butt till he was propped up on a nearby tree. There was no cover here from that helicopter and he looked around himself for any kind of shelter. The wolf was circling him keeping her head pointed away from him. Did she know how injured he was? He lifted himself on his good left leg into a standing position. Keeping his right leg propped away from his body he hopped on his good leg away from the tree. He needed to find a place to hide and rest. The pain in his leg would go away; he just needed a few hours rest. Just then his foot slapped up against the tree and the pain almost blinded him. Maybe it would take more than just a few hours.

He looked around himself and didn't see anything that would give them any shelter at all. He looked down at his companion. "You wouldn't happen to know of a place where we could rest for the night?" The wolf turned to look at him. He could see himself reflected in those golden eyes. She lowered her head toward his outstretched foot. She prodded it gently with her nose. He bit down on his lower lip as more pain surged through his body. Hearing his groan she whimpered in sympathy, at least that's what it sounded like to him.

The wolf turned and slowly walked off a little deeper into the woods. He did his best to hop after her. This was ridiculous. There was nothing wrong with his leg and yet every time he put any kind of pressure on it, he almost fell because of the pain. *Maybe it is broken.*

The wolf led him back into the forest and he was leaning heavily on the surrounding trees for support. The wolf jogged ahead of him. He tried to make himself move faster but his useless foot did everything it could to hamper his progress and he was forced to hobble along at a cripple's pace.

The wolf disappeared from his view, but he wasn't worried. He knew that she would be back shortly. All he could do was move along as fast as he was able. He rested for a time against a large redwood. He could smell the bark and the earth around him. It was a comforting feeling being surrounded by the forest. This is where he belonged, this was home. Of course, he had never had an injury like this. What was he going to do if his ankle was in fact more injured than he wanted to admit? He would worry about that eventuality when it was a reality. For right now he was only concerned with moving.

He moved away from the tree trunk and hopped where the she-wolf had disappeared from his vision. He had trouble following her trail through the underbrush. Every branch that swept past his foot was a brush with pain that he wished he could do without. The pain was subsiding slowly, but he was still unable to put any pressure on it. He looked around at the sky and the old man was lower than he expected. *The sun will set in a few hours.* He had to find some shelter before that and he quickened his pace, as much as he could.

After a while, the wolf came trotting back to him and, staying only a few feet in front of him, led him off to the west. The sun was very low in the sky. The wolf was ahead of him trotting along without much concern, though her head was always moving back and forth, and her ears were listening to everything. She was aware of what was happening around her, but she continued forward with no rush whatsoever.

He admired the animal's pure survival instincts. She knew that he was injured and that he couldn't move or fight so to compensate for that loss of support she moved slower and was listening more intently to the world around her. She was preparing to defend herself and him at any time. She knew that he wasn't going to be much use in a fight and had taken the full responsibility of their safety on her shoulders.

The cramp in his side hadn't gone away and every hop he took jolted his side and sent continuous waves of pain along his body. He had tried to tense his muscles to stabilize his side and his foot, but that hadn't done anything except use up energy. So, he just had to live with the pain till they reached wherever the wolf was leading him.

The wolf trotted away from him again. She stopped and turned around looking at him waiting for him to catch up. The sun had started to dip under the horizon, and he hoped that wherever the wolf had decided to make shelter for the night was close by. He hopped toward the wolf and saw where she had led him.

The place could be described as a thicket, or a hell hole with brambles. He was standing in front of a massive tangle of thorns and bushes. "You've got to be kidding."

9

The wolf lowered herself, dug out a small hole, and disappeared under the briars and thorns. He closed his eyes and sighed deeply. *The good thing is nobody will think to look for me under there. The bad thing is I might lose a pint of blood or two just getting in and out of that hole.*

The wolf did not come back out. Sighing, he turned around and lowered himself onto his butt. Being careful not to jostle his foot and keep it as stationary as possible he scooted backward toward the brambles. Lifting his whole body with his arms and using his good left leg, he pushed himself backward. When he was close to the hole he laid back and pushed himself under the thorns with his left leg.

The thorns passed over him scraping his vest and face. He turned his head to protect his eyes and face. It was a tight space, but he was able to keep moving using his leg and hands to slowly propel himself through the passageway. The thorns raised themselves and soon he was able to bend his leg more and he didn't have to keep his head turned. The tunnel that he was traveling was expanding while the brambles above him grew denser.

This place was turning out to be pretty cool. As he moved deeper into the briar patch, he found that he had more and more room to maneuver his body. The pain in his side and ankle were still there but they were ebbing, and he was certain that after a good night's sleep both the cramp in his side and his tender ankle would be back to normal by sunrise.

It had become darker in the briars, and he knew that the sun had set. As he moved along, the tunnel of briars opened up to become a clearing. He twisted himself around and found that the wolf was there watching him. There was enough room here for her to sit up straight. The ceiling of thorns was a good three to four feet off the ground and he was able to sit up as well without fear of cutting himself.

He pulled his right leg to himself and started massaging his hurt ankle. The pain was not nearly as intense as it had been, but it was still too painful to walk. The wolf lowered her head toward his injury and sniffed at his ankle. She moved closer to the injury sniffing while she neared his bare skin. With his hand massaging his ankle, he watched as the wolf got closer to his foot. *Sometimes she acts like a domesticated pet.* But he knew better than to completely lower his guard around her. Even so, he let her get closer to his foot. She lunged forward and snapped at his leg just above his hurt ankle.

He yelled in surprise. It hadn't hurt, not really, but he was not expecting her to do that. He let go of his foot and swatted at her. "What the hell did you do that for?" The she-wolf ducked away from the slap and backed away from him till her back was up against a wall of thorns. He moved toward her to make sure he could get some satisfaction. He was not going to let a wolf or anything else get away with snapping at him.

As he tried to maneuver his body toward the wolf, he noticed that the pain coming from his ankle had dissipated. He stopped and reached for his foot. He tucked his right leg toward him and looked at the small red mark that the wolf had left. There wasn't even a bite mark, just some red irritation that would fade in a few minutes. He massaged his ankle and found that the pain was almost entirely gone. He looked at the wolf in amazement.

"How did you do that?"

The she-wolf looked at him. She sat on her haunches, every inch of her a proud predator. She looked like an enforcer who had just returned home from some great battle after killing many people. Her eyes didn't waver from his. It wasn't a look of submission, but it wasn't a challenge either. She just sat there watching him.

He looked back down at his foot and made it rotate. There was almost no pain whatsoever. He placed his foot down on the ground and using his arms for balance he lifted his body off the ground. With his back parallel to the ground and his foot bearing his weight he stretched out his back and tested his ankle. His foot supported him with little problem. He lowered his body back down to the ground. He looked up into the thorns overhead. They were so dense that he couldn't see the sky or the forest above him. He took a deep breath and rolled over onto his stomach. He lifted his body, swung his legs out from under him, and landed in a sitting position facing the wolf.

"I'm sorry I swatted at you." The wolf sat there looking at him making no movement toward, or away from him. "You surprised me. I didn't know you were trying to help me. All I knew is that a, no offense, a wild animal had just bitten me for no reason."

The wolf cocked her head to the side as he said 'wild animal.' She turned away from him and started digging in the ground. She moved the disturbed soil and retrieved the buried piece of denim that she had carried over the last few days. She took the piece of fabric in her mouth. She walked toward him and dropped the denim at his feet. He looked at her and she backed away from him. He picked up the faded, moist piece of blue fabric and held it in his hands. "I don't understand." He was troubled by the gesture. The wolf lay down on her stomach. His brow furrowed as he studied the fabric and his companion. He looked from one then the other. *Did I insult you in some way? Did wolves get insulted?* She certainly seemed to be pissed off at him.

"What did I say?"

The wolf shifted her gaze away from him and stared out at the thorns.

"Look, I said I'm sorry. What more do you want me to do?"

The wolf lifted her head and looked at him. She did not growl, nor did she bare her teeth at him. She just looked at him and, in that look, he understood, somehow. The hurt that she conveyed in that wilting look would have melted a jaguar. She dropped her head to rest on her legs that were spread out in front of her. She turned her head back to the briar wall leaving him to deal with his guilt alone.

He started to apologize once more but he knew that it was not going to do any good. In fact, it might insult her further. He lowered his eyes down to the dirty piece of fabric that he was holding. He couldn't see any damage to the ripped pair of shorts except the whole being ripped-in-half thing. He took out the other half of the shorts that he had carried with him inside his pants. He held both pieces of fabric together. He looked over at the wolf. She looked like she was asleep. He knew she wasn't.

He kept his eyes on her until he could barely make out the outline of her body against the deep surrounding shadows. From behind she was covered with only softly textured black fur, almost impossible to see in the deepening dark that fell around them. He didn't know if she was sleeping or not. He looked at her for a long time before a light, fitful, guilt-riddled sleep took over him.

He awoke at the sound of helicopter blades. The helicopter was close, much closer than he would have liked. If it was the same helicopter that they escaped earlier, it was traveling much slower and much lower to the ground. He jerked himself up and looked around. The she-wolf was already at work digging under the briars of the enclosure. He wondered why she was digging. The noise from the helicopter was loud and he knew that it was close by. But even its searchlight wouldn't be able to penetrate the thorns that enclosed them.

He moved over to the she-wolf. His ankle was fine even after so little sleep. He moved it, rotated it, and put his weight on it. There was no pain and no sign that anything had happened to it. The noise from the rotor blades was deafening even though they were insulated from it by the briar patch. He moved beside the wolf. He lifted his hand to pet her but before his hands came above her head she snarled and whipped her head toward him. She bared her teeth at him and growled. Her snout was about three inches away from his face and he could see death in her golden eyes. He withdrew his hands from her head, and she turned back to her work. The helicopter had either entered into a hover, or it was moving at a snail's pace because the noise of its rotor blades wasn't getting any softer, but it wasn't getting any louder either. His mind reeled in panic. Did they find us? How did they find us? What would they do when they finally caught them?

The she-wolf obviously wasn't ready to be captured yet and she was working on an escape route. If those guys in the helicopter had tracked them here then they had followed their trail into the briar patch, so the tunnel they had used to get here was not an option. Now he understood why the wolf was digging under the thorns. They had to get out another way.

He dove beside her and shoved his hands in the rich dark soil, moving handfuls away from the hole that the she-wolf was digging. Those guys probably had people on the ground and if they were in a military helicopter, it only stood to reason that they would have military personnel on the ground looking for them. Those military personnel would be armed.

He dug more. If the helicopter was still hovering, and the sound hadn't changed for a minute or two, then that would mean the ground assets hadn't arrived yet. They still had some time, but he had no idea how much time. His hands became bloody from scraping up against the thorns that he was digging under.

Time was moving too quickly. They didn't have any time. Any minute some soldier would poke his head through the entrance tunnel and order them to stop, or just shoot them both in the back. His mind was in a blind panic. *What do they want from me?* He was sweating with the exertion of the work but also from fear and the phantom soldiers that would shoot him any second. He almost cried out for nothing else than to drown out the noise of the helicopter.

He dug faster but it wasn't fast enough. Too much time had passed.

Just when he thought his phantoms would drive him insane, he could see a small opening leading out of the briar patch. The she-wolf lowered herself and scrambled through the hole. He turned around and saw the two pieces of denim in the dirt where he had left them. If those government guys had tracked him here, then there was no reason to keep the fabric. But he picked them up anyway and stuffed them into his pants. Turning toward the hole he dove after the wolf.

The briars grabbed at him and dug into his back. He fought and kicked his way through the hole into the open forest. The night air was dark and cold. He would have looked up for the stars but the searchlight from the helicopter outshined all the stars and filled the would-be somber atmosphere with its loud mechanical sound that he could barely hear himself think. He put his hands to his ears and dove behind a tree as the searchlight passed over where he and the wolf had escaped from the briar patch.

He was panting from fear and uncertainty. He knew he had to get away, but he couldn't outrun a helicopter to say nothing of outrunning a bullet. He got up and moved from tree to tree trying to get an idea of what was happening around him. His worst fears were realized as he heard men yelling at each other over the din of the rotor blades. They were closer than he realized, and he almost gave up hope.

Just when he was ready to make a break for it the she-wolf returned to his side. She rammed her head into his leg and the slight pain was enough to clear his mind from the paralyzing fear that had gripped him. The wolf moved off into the forest, moving along the tree's shadows and moving away from the briar patch. He followed her and, aided by the helicopter's flood lights, they were able to move at almost full speed through the night.

His ankle didn't bother him at all, and he was soon moving at the speeds that they had traveled yesterday. His heightened sense of awareness kept the hairs on the back of his neck raised and he was sure that any second a shot would ring out and he would fall to the ground, pierced by a sniper shot.

He wasn't stupid enough to lower his guard or slow down. With the helicopter falling farther behind them, he started to get a feeling of where they were going. He couldn't be sure in the deep darkness of night, but he felt like they were running southward the way they had come the previous day. The wolf might be following the trail they made yesterday. If these people followed their trail to the briar patch, they would almost certainly follow them back here and hopefully, they would be stuck in the endless loop that his guide was leaving for them. He marveled at the sheer intelligence of this wolf. He might have been able to think about doing something like that eventually but the fear and the panic that had gripped him so completely had blinded him. He would have run aimlessly till he was caught.

Just when he was about to breathe a sigh of relief at their escape, he heard a sharp cry pierce the relative quiet out here away from that devil machine. It was a bloodthirsty howl, but it hadn't come from any wolf. His mind reached back to when he had run with his pack. The howl hadn't come from any coyote either. That howl had come from a dog. He thought about how long it would take for those guys to find them.

The dog's howl split the night sky and he added more speed as he ran after his guide. He may not be able to run from them forever, but he wasn't going to just give up because of a dog either. He was a werewolf, King of the Forest, alpha to his pack and he would never surrender to anything, especially not to those who would hunt him down like a dog in his home.

He poured more and more speed into his legs. Wherever the she-wolf was leading him he hoped that she had accounted for the possibility of being tracked by other animals. He had lost faith in her once and she had saved him time and time again, he would not lose faith in her twice.

They continued to run, and he became more and more convinced that they were in fact moving south. The sound of the helicopter had faded but not disappeared. *It must be following us.* But it wasn't traveling at even a tenth of its potential. It was possible that the helicopter was moving just ahead of the ground units using its flood light as a screen for the actual hunting party.

They continued to put distance between themselves and the sound of the helicopter. They heard the howl once more, but it was much farther off than it had been before. He allowed his mind to wonder where the she-wolf was taking them. They were backtracking where they had traveled yesterday, of that much he was fairly certain. But where were they going?

His eyes widened in surprise as his mind caught on the answer. *The creek.* Of course, the she-wolf was leading him back to the creek that they had stopped at to wash after their breakfast yesterday. The dogs wouldn't be able to track them through the water. The creek would be deep enough to hide their scent but shallow enough for them to run in for a while. With the speed that they were capable of it would take these guys several days to pick up the scent again if the creek ran for any distance.

They ran for a long while, a lot longer than he remembered running yesterday. The sound of the helicopter was almost gone from the night air, but he didn't allow himself to slow down. His guide kept pace with him, but she wasn't slowing down either, her lead was pushing him to maintain their current breakneck speed.

After some time, they reached the creek. He could see the moonlight being reflected off the water's surface. He didn't have time to admire his mother though. The wolf splashed into the creek and slowing only a fraction, she ran upstream toward the east. He crashed into the water behind her and followed her along the creek bed.

The bottom of the creek was mostly sand, and his toes squished into it as he ran. He slowed down as he had to work harder just to pick his feet up and out of the grasping sand and the surrounding water that came up to just below his knees. The wolf was still running but her speed had slowed as well. They had put a good deal of distance between them and the pursuing men and dogs, but that distance would shrink very quickly if they couldn't get some of their speed back. Unfortunately, they had to stay in the water otherwise their escape would be tracked by those dogs and everything they had worked for so far tonight would be for nothing.

They struggled through the water as best as they could. The helicopter was getting louder, and they heard the dog's howl again much closer than it had been the last time they had heard it. He dug his feet into the creek bed and forced himself to run faster. The wolf had adapted to the new terrain and was leaping up out of the water every other step. She was traveling faster and faster as she became used to the new way of moving. He just gritted his teeth and forced his legs to move faster and higher, taking his feet out of the water entirely. Their speed was nothing like what it was on solid ground, but it was improving, and they were making a fair amount of progress.

It didn't take long for the helicopter and the pursuing dogs to reach the creek. By that time, they had traveled a good mile, mile and a half, up creek and were still gathering speed. He could tell the helicopter had reached the creek because the sound of the blades had stopped moving. The helicopter and pursuing agents were not stupid. The helicopter noise faded even more, and he knew that the helicopter was following the creek deeper in the forest.

That had been as good a guess as any. Why would a fugitive from the federal government run toward the open expanse of the mountains? It made a lot more sense for him to run deeper into the woods hoping to lose them in the forest. He might have come to that conclusion as well, but his guide had turned east, and he was grateful for the fifty/fifty decision that she had made. For the time being it had proven itself to be the right choice.

They continued to struggle with the depth of the water. Their speed increased for a time but was slowed by the varying depths of the creek. They were moving faster than a normal person could move in the creek, but it was still no match for a helicopter or even for people who were running on land. It was still very dark, so he didn't have to worry about agents tracking him without the telltale noise of the helicopter and its bright flood lights. They continued to move upstream toward the mountains.

They ran through the water and out of the forest. When the trees finally gave way to the bare rock of the mountain once again, they left the cold water of the creek. His legs, even though they had been working hard for the last hour or so, were chilled to the bone. He was glad to be out of the water so he could allow feeling to return to his feet. The wolf didn't hesitate for a second and took off running along the open rock.

The moon was almost cut in half. Even in this phase, her brilliance was unquestionable. She shone down just enough to allow him and his guide to see where they were going. The wolf did not hesitate a moment and ran eastward following the creek. He didn't quite understand this logic, but he wouldn't question her now. They ran along the rock, her footsteps were as quiet as a shadow, while doing his best to be silent, he could still hear the slight slapping of his bare feet on the rock. He tried to quiet his steps in the still night but nothing he tried helped to diminish the sound of his footsteps. He soon gave up on trying to suppress it and just concentrated on running.

They were running along an incline in the mountain and soon the terrain was not smooth or even. They had to slow down as they entered the higher altitudes of the mountain. Now they were in the crags and crevices of the mountain. No person had ever tried to scale or traverse these small winding passes, and he hoped that fact would deter any pursuit this way. They had good cover from ground level. But being on bare rock they were still very susceptible to being spotted from the air. His mind caught on to the idea that a helicopter could only fly so high, about ten thousand feet. If they could get higher than ten thousand feet that should remove the advantage of their pursuers.

He slapped himself in the face for being so stupid. *If we could get that high, we would be waist-deep in snow. You'd freeze to death with only that vest on, or did you forget that you are hopelessly unprepared for winter?* OK, so they couldn't take the high ground. The only thing for him to do was move at pace with his guide and trust that she knew where she was going.

After they had entered the crags of the mountain the wolf turned north once again, and they were moving faster. He had to use all his concentration on seeing the ground and not getting his feet caught in the sharp rocks. He looked westward for a moment and saw that his mother was lower in the sky than he had hoped. Morning would be coming soon. The sky hadn't begun to lighten yet, but he knew that soon the east sky would begin to paint itself with the reds and oranges of sunrise and the morning.

Running perpendicular to the setting moon they moved northward at dangerous speeds. He barely avoided serious injuries several times, but the wolf didn't slow. She was pushing him harder than she had ever done before. Granted, they had never been so close to being captured either, but he hadn't heard any trace of the helicopter for a few hours now. And nobody could or would move through these mountains at the speeds that they were traveling at. All these facts were lost on the wolf, however, and she kept her pace like she was running away from a nightmare.

He was using his arms as much as he was his legs. The narrow passes that they were moving through were high and he could use his arms for leverage through the difficult terrain. He wouldn't be able to see the sunrise from deep within the crevices and boulders that they were passing through, but he didn't need to. Somehow, he knew that his mother had finally set. When he looked up, the sky was already fading from black to blue. It was going to be a great day. *Yeah, a great day. If you just ignore the fact that guys with dogs and a military helicopter are trying to hunt us down, we could probably take a break and sunbathe for a while.* Sometimes his own sarcastic nature got the better of him and he grimaced at the prospect of being captured. The wolf had opened the distance between them while he was lost in himself, and he had to work twice as hard to catch back up to her.

The sun reached its zenith and looked down to find them still moving at impossibly dangerous speeds along the razor-sharp crags and crevices of the mountain. Through the morning, he had not heard the helicopter again nor had he heard any howls from pursuing dogs. Surely those agents must have figured out that they had followed the creek in the wrong direction. They had to have backtracked and followed the creek eastward by now. The helicopter had, in all likelihood, gone back to wherever it was based out of to refuel. He had no idea how far away that would be or how safe that made them.

The air was getting colder, and he could only guess that they were moving higher as well as going north. The wolf was running with an untiring iron will that impressed him thoroughly. *Is she still mad at me?* He hadn't thought about the insult since he had woken up last night, but now, as he was settling into the familiar rhythm of following his guide, his mind was able to drift and it brought him back to last night. *What had I said that insulted her so badly?* He decided to just let it rest and not worry about it. He had apologized for what he had said and if she was still going to be sore at him for it, well, that would be dealt with later. That didn't stop him from feeling guilty about it though. He had to make it up to her somehow. If she had been human, he could have bought her flowers but what on earth could wolves want that she couldn't get for herself? He shook his head and followed his guide northward.

After some time had passed, they came to a dark low-ceilinged tunnel. He could just make out the light at the end of it. The light shining through the opening at the end of the tunnel was no bigger than a small fly. The tunnel was dark and long. It would shield them from the sun as well as any unwelcome visitors from the sky.

He sat down opposite his companion near the opening of the cave, where the light of the late afternoon was filtering into the dark space allowing them to see without difficulty. She sat bolt upright with her head toward the entrance of the cave. She wasn't going to let her guard down. If she had been human, he would have sworn that she was intentionally avoiding looking at him.

He looked at her. "I'm sorry if whatever I said upset you." The wolf didn't acknowledge him or that he had spoken at all. "I've tried to remember but I can't remember exactly what I said." He lowered his head knowing that he was not getting anywhere with his companion. She continued to look out over the mountain crags and crevices that they had traversed to get here to this cave.

He raised his blue-green eyes. "You saved me last night. I know that this doesn't mean much but I'm sorry for whatever I said last night. I said it without thinking, which is probably why I can't remember it." He shook his head. If anybody else could see him trying to talk to a wolf and apologize to her for something that he said, that she probably couldn't understand, he would be laughed at for the rest of his life. But that is precisely the reason why had left all those people behind to live among the animals and nature in the first place.

He leaned toward her. "I'm sorry."

The wolf remained rigid, with her gaze fixed outside the cave. For a moment he thought that the wolf would snub him once again. He looked at her, pleading with her through his eyes, and she made the smallest movement of her head. That movement brought her eyes to lock onto his and he saw her nod her head ever so slightly. She turned back toward the cave entrance, and he leaned back against the tunnel wall. He knew in that glance that she had forgiven him, but the incident would not go unremembered.

It was late afternoon and soon the old man would set, leaving his mother to take her place. That was good. The night would be cool, and they would be able to move a little more freely. The men pursuing them would have to have the helicopter's light to search and the sound of the machine would give them all the warning they needed. He knew he should get some sleep while he could. The wolf would probably want to move as soon as the sun set.

The she-wolf sat, still watching and listening, at the entrance of the tunnel. Looking at her he was struck with just how beautiful an animal she was. She had a sleek, shiny coat of black fur, and her gold eyes were intense and alert. She had kept him safe and led him to this spot away from their pursuers.

He rested his head against the cool rock of the tunnel. He could sleep easy knowing that she was watching and guarding him. He shifted his butt around on the rock floor till he was as comfortable as he was going to get. He looked down toward the exit of the tunnel. Looking into the darkness with that small hole of light at the end gave him some comfort. They had an escape route should they require it.

He allowed his eyes to close. He felt safer now than he probably had any right to feel. His she-wolf companion was keeping watch and he felt comfortable. The solid rock under and behind him cooled his worn body through his skins and he drifted off to sleep.

He was running through his forest. He had changed and his powerful werewolf form was taking him easily over the land. He was eating distances, and he felt no pain, no fatigue, just the pure joy of the hunt. He was surrounded by his pack, and they were running downhill. He looked to his right and keeping pace with him there was the old grey wolf that he had defeated so long ago. The grey was running with his tongue hanging out. Not very dignified for a wolf, but he knew the grey was just enjoying the run.

He looked to his left and running ahead of him and gaining speed was the black she-wolf. He could make out her white starburst on her chest. She looked back at him, the familiar piece of denim hanging from her mouth. He gave a short bark. The bark was repeated by the old grey and soon the entire pack was barking. The sound filled the night forest. He smiled and ran faster. They were the kings of the night, and the forest was their playground. No one and nothing would challenge them here. He was the alpha and the pack was safe. He felt the pure rush of joy surge through him, a joy at being free that very few humans would ever feel.

He led the pack around a boulder and off to the right. He knew the river was just ahead and he wanted to hit the ford at a dead run. The water that would be splashed up by him and his pack was always amazing. With his wolf sight, he could make out the river through the trees. He smiled and howled as he crashed through the underbrush and ripped through the calm moving river ford.

His pack was strangely silent, but it didn't register to him. He was lost in the intricate sounds of every water droplet as it splashed back down into the river. The symphony that the water and he made was beautiful. Each drop made its own unique sound and pitch as it sprayed his fur, or pinged off the nearby rocks, or as it splashed back down into the river itself. It was like listening to a thousand different wind chimes all at once.

He crossed the river in a few long strides. His smile froze on his face as he realized that none of his pack had crossed with him. He skidded to a halt and looked back. His pack was stumbling and hobbling toward him. His eyes brought him horrors that he wished he couldn't see. The old grey clearly had a broken leg, and his hind left leg was missing. The bloody stump where his leg should have been was trailing a grotesque amount of blood behind him. His one good eye looked up at him. He could see unbearable pain but also, he saw the unspoken accusations of the grey as he hobbled toward the river. The grey was dying, and he blamed it on him. In his mind, he heard the wolf speak to him in a gruff, muffled, pain-filled voice. He had never heard this voice before, but he knew it to be the old grey wolf speaking to him.

'You did this to me,' the grey was saying. 'When we needed you most you disappeared and left us to the mercy of those humans.' The grey was walking slower but determination would not let him stop. 'You were our alpha and you abandoned us.'

He reeled back in agony as the voice was joined by others.

'You left us to fend for ourselves.'

'What good are claws and teeth against guns?'

'How could we have known?'

He fell to his knees at the mental bombardment. He held his head in his hands as tears fell freely from his eyes. "I didn't know. How could I have known this was going to happen?"

His pack, mangled and half dead, continued to walk toward him, their blood staining the ground behind them.

He saw the black she-wolf with the white starburst on her chest. She was sitting upright on a rock on the far side riverbank. She was looking at him with hatred in her eyes. She was accusing him as well. She spit the denim from her mouth into the river and the river turned a frothy red with the blood that had soaked through the material.

He watched the piece of denim float down the river and then looked at the she-wolf again. What was hidden behind the piece of fabric that was now exposed was a charred hole in the middle of her chest. He could see her heart slowly beating and the white of her ribcage. Blood flowed freely from the wound and ran into the river.

'You left us.'

'You abandoned us.'

'We died because you weren't here.'

'You're no alpha.'

'Deceiver.'

'Usurper.'

His pack continued to drag their wounded and dying bodies toward him and he knew what they wanted. They were coming for him. Without the pack, the alpha is nothing. Without the alpha, the pack is nothing. He had left them without a leader, without direction. Now, they would exact their price for their pain. They would take payment for their lives with his.

Tears streamed from his eyes as he stumbled to the middle of the river ford. "I'm sorry. Please forgive me." He sank to his knees in the cold water. He begged for forgiveness, but his pack was not in a forgiving mood. The old grey was ahead of the other mangled wolves. The river water was red with their blood. He left himself open and the old grey lunged at his exposed neck.

He barked out a cry of pain. Another wolf lunged at his

outstretched arms. If the wolf had been a little stronger, he would have ripped his arm clean out of its socket. He howled in pain as the rest of the pack descended on him ripping and biting into him. Their claws and razor-sharp teeth tore into his exposed flesh. He looked down in horror as he saw he was no longer in werewolf form but his frail, pink, painful human form. He cried out as the pack pulled him off his knees and ripped into him, his back pinned down on the frigid riverbed. He looked up reaching out for something or someone. Sitting there on the riverbed rock, not having moved at all, was the black and white she-wolf. She was watching him being torn to pieces and he saw her smile down at him in the moonlight.

10

Kenneth was losing his patience with these so-called law enforcement agents. He once again found himself in Mark's office. These trips to the State Trooper Station were getting tedious. They had him, again they had found him, and somehow, against all logic, William Setford had managed to evade them. A damn helicopter can't be expected to track this kid through some trees and mountains?!

"Mark, why can't we seem to eliminate a single, twenty something year old boy? Do you need more funding for better training? Am I not being clear enough with my intent on exactly how important it is that this dangerous murderer be found and brought to justice?" Kenneth asked evenly.

Mark looked across the desk at the vampire as the smug, hoity toity little ass hole steepled his fingertips in that annoying prissy prick way of his. Mark had a feeling that if he actually voiced any of those thoughts, he would end up dead in seconds. "I am trying to find out why," Mark said instead. "That mountainous terrain isn't easy to traverse. The helicopter only has so much fuel and can only do so much on one trip. And if we put any more resources on this, you know people in places that you and I don't want scrutiny from, will start asking questions we don't want asked."

Kenneth sat stewing in his chair. This was getting ridiculous. He knew that Mark wasn't wrong. He had run the numbers himself on just what he would be able to use, and what would go unnoticed. But the fact that they had been close, or at least they said they had been close, twice, and they came back empty handed both times? This was starting to push even his supernatural patience.

Mark closed his eyes and leaned back in his chair massaging the bridge of his nose. He leaned down to pull open one of his lower desk drawers and pulled out a vacuum sealed, clear plastic package. Kenneth saw inside was what looked like mostly grey fur.

"And that is?" Kenneth asked.

Mark smiled, "Well we did have some good news, our killer might still be on the loose, but our hunters ran into a bit of luck in that valley. They already got one wolf and the pelt has already been cleaned and prepped, just for you." Mark handed the plastic pouch over to the vampire. "I don't have to tell you that my guys were really motivated and excited to get as much of those bounties you promised as possible, and are tearing that valley apart looking for more wolves for you."

Kenneth turned the vacuum sealed plastic over in his hands. Inside the plastic, the fur was clean and looked almost majestic.

"Ah, yes the two thousand dollars per pelt," Kenneth finally said. "Your hunters will get their bounty, rest assured."

Mark's expression soured, "Two thousand? Uh, Mr. Pacifico you said three thousand."

Kenneth knowing full well what he had said, let a dark look pass over his eyes at being called out. But it wouldn't do to push things, the wolves were being taken care of, that was worth the extra money out of his pocket. "So be it, three thousand for each pelt. So long as every last one of them is exterminated."

Kenneth left the office and did the quick math. Getting rid of a couple dozen wolves was always worth it, but did he really have to promise a hundred thousand dollars for it? It was a knee jerk promise, something he made with no thought as to how that might actually stack up against his bank account. Just so long as that valley was free of wolves, it would be worth it. Less chance for those filthy barbarian werewolves to reproduce and thrive right under his nose.

11

William screamed in pain as he jerked himself awake and shoved himself away from the cool tunnel wall. He gripped at his body. No blood. His arms were still in place. His legs, though drenched in sweat, were fine and he moved them gently to test for damage. He felt at his face. His nose wasn't broken, and his eyes were not oozing anything. He took several deep breaths and looked out of the tunnel at the rapidly darkening sky. It was quickly becoming night. He saw the she-wolf. She was still at the mouth of the tunnel, but she had laid down to sleep as well. His scream must have woken her because she was looking right at him. She didn't get up but looked at him with her head cocked to one side. *Do wolves know what nightmares are?* He rubbed at his face and his strained eyes. He ran his hands over the whole of his body as he took deep breaths to calm down.

His mind came back to reality, and he slowly made himself remember that he was still inside the tunnel that the she-wolf had led him to. He had been traveling with a black and white she-wolf for a few days now. He had escaped that briar patch when the she-wolf had heard the helicopter blades and dug a way for them to escape even though he had insulted her a few hours before. That brought an uncomfortable twinge of guilt upon him that he didn't like. She had forgiven him but there was something in the way that she had forgiven him that made him slightly uneasy. She wanted something other than a simple apology, but what? As he watched the she-wolf get up and stretch her body, he tried to remember what exactly he had said to offend her so badly.

His heart was still racing. He clutched at his chest and forced his heart rate to slow. He was still shaken by the nightmare, and he had trouble concentrating. His eyes adjusted to the darkening tunnel as the world prepared for night. He sighed deeply and wiped at his face and eyes. His breathing was ragged and uneven. He tried to calm down, but the images of his pack mangled and dying danced in front of his vision with no sign of relenting.

He shook his head and stood up. Stifling a yawn, he turned around and pressed his head against the cool stone. What had caused him to dream of that? In the time he had lived in the wild, he hadn't had one nightmare. So why had he been having them so regularly as of late and why did he have to experience one now that was such a horrible vision that no man should have to witness?

His mind turned back to his pack. They had survived without him for years. He only led them on the nights of full moons. The old grey would take care of them. 'Usurper' they had called him. Because he had defeated the old grey in combat, did that mean the grey saw himself as no longer fit to lead the pack? He shook his head. There was nothing he could do about that now. He was being hunted; they were not. If he went back to his valley, it would accomplish nothing except put his pack in danger.

The visions would not get out of his head, and he growled loudly building into a scream. The she-wolf raised her head at the sudden sound. She looked concerned but also angry. That look screamed at him. 'Are you crazy?' For the first time in a long time, he was scared. Scared for his pack and scared for himself and his companion. What if the cops did do something horrible to his pack while he was away? Now he knew what Luke Skywalker felt like on Dagobah. "I can't get these visions out of my head. They're my friends I've got to help them." *And look what happened to him, he lost his hand, and he wasn't able to save Han anyway.* He knew that it was a dream, but something had felt terrible, and he knew that there was something different about this dream than normal dreams. There really was nothing for him to do. He had to keep following his guide. She had been in the dream too and there was a meaning behind all of it.

He put his hands up on the rock wall and stretched his legs and body. His mouth cracked a huge yawn. His nap had done very little to refresh him but that couldn't be helped. His method of waking up hadn't pleased his companion but they both knew that they had been in this place for too long.

He turned back toward his companion, who was already moving toward the far end of the tunnel. The sun's light was all but gone from the world, and the tunnel was already pitch black. He followed his guide more by sound and feel than by sight. His time in nature had refined both senses; even so, he moved his feet out in front of him. He couldn't hear his guide as she walked, but he could hear the sounds of the tunnel and a slight whistling sound as the wind moved through the tunnel.

The light at the end of the tunnel was nothing more now than a slight smudge of lesser black against the void of darkness that they were now walking. He wished he could move faster. The floor of the tunnel was relatively even, and he tried to make his feet and legs move more quickly. He didn't know where his guide was. For all he knew she could be at the other end of the tunnel by now. Would she leave him here, alone in the darkness? Would she leave him to fend for himself? His mind started to panic, and he begged his body for more speed. His body stubbornly remained moving at the same slow pace.

He knew to ensure his health and safety he couldn't move any faster but that didn't stop him from wanting to break out in a dead run toward that smudge of darkness that was the tunnel exit. His breathing was getting shorter and shallower. His vision blurred as a cold sweat broke out on his forehead. He was afraid. The nightmare had awakened fears in him that he hadn't even realized he had. He was afraid for his pack. He was afraid for his companion. If those agents caught them, she would probably be shot on sight as he was taken into custody. He was afraid that he had slept too long, and that those agents would be waiting for them outside the tunnel. He would have traversed this hellish void only to be blinded by that helicopter's flood light as it drowned him in its bright artificial light. Then agents with dogs would surround him and order him to the ground. The she-wolf wouldn't go down without a fight and she would lunge at the nearest dog tearing into its neck. An agent would shove a shotgun barrel under her neck and pull the trigger spraying her life blood and guts all over the surrounding rock.

He wanted to scream.

He wanted to do something to drown out these images

that kept assaulting his mind in the black of this death trap that he willingly entered. He was getting lightheaded as the darkness swirled around him. If he didn't get a hold of himself, he was going to pass out. He tried in vain, and the fear continued to grip him, driving all reason from his mind.

Just when he thought he must go insane from the images that assaulted him he felt a warm presence brush up against his leg. He jumped back and away from the unknown form in a purely fight-or-flight reflex. He couldn't see, but he knew that the form was the she-wolf. She pressed her body against his leg rubbing up against his furs. He reached down and put a shaky hand on top of her head. He felt her thick fur through his fingertips, and he felt her warmth.

He kept his hand there for a moment, unmoving then he removed it from her body. She pressed up against him moving and aiding him. His fear dissipated from him, and he was able to calm down and get control of his breathing. He took several deep breaths and cleansed his mind from the images and the fear that he had let get the better of him.

The wolf moved away from him, but he could still feel her presence. He could hear a barely audible clicking bounce off the tunnel walls around him. It took him a moment to figure out that it was the wolf's claws upon the rock floor that was making the sound. Every few steps he could hear the soft click of wolf claw against rock. The sound was reassuring and the fear that had gripped him so thoroughly a few moments before did not threaten him again.

They exited the tunnel a lot sooner than he had expected. The exit was smaller than the entrance and the forced perspective that he had viewed the exit made it seem a lot farther away than it actually was. They stepped through the small opening in the rock and breathed in the cool, open night air. The stars were shining, and the moon was less than half of her true brilliance. He was struck with a sense of deep sadness seeing his mother wane like this. It was a feeling of deep melancholy that he just couldn't seem to explain or shrug off. He had never felt this way when he was living in society but looking at his mother fail in the night sky was like watching someone he loved die. It happened every time she was this weak. He knew better than that. His mother wasn't going anywhere and it was nothing more than the earth's rotation. That her shape was nothing more than where sunlight happened to reflect off her surface. Still, he couldn't help what he felt, and no amount of logic could ease that sense of loss.

The wolf had sat down beside him, and her head was moving back and forth, searching. Her deep eyes were looking out over the mountain. Neither he nor his companion could hear any sign of pursuit. She had her ears cocked ever so slightly and he knew that she was listening for the things that he couldn't hear.

She must have been satisfied with her investigation because she began to move in the darkness away from the tunnel. She wound her way through the boulders and crevices that made up the path that they now tread, and he followed her.

His eyes had adjusted as much as they were able to in the night's darkness. The path the wolf was leading him through was deep and the night's gentle light didn't pene-trate to the mountain rock on which they now traveled. His feet were covered in deep shadows, and he was unsure of his footing. He had to travel much slower than they had been able to the previous night, but it was still faster than he had been forced to move while inside that tunnel.

Using his hands for support against the rock wall he let his feet probe in front of him. It was a taxing process, but it was the only way to ensure that he didn't impale his feet on the sharp rocks of the mountain. He couldn't see anything more than five feet in front of him. The path was winding and twisting. The wolf was never more than two steps in front of him though, and he felt comforted by her presence.

The wind did not relent in these deep passages of rock. Its swift movement was stealing his body heat as it whistled through the deep channels of rock. He began to shiver. His mother was of no comfort, and he knew that the cold was only going to get worse. Winter was getting closer and as they continued to move northward and higher up into the mountain the sun's influence would weaken more and more. Of course, the sun had nothing to do with the night. The night was its own province and he started to wonder if he would make it to wherever the wolf was leading him.

As if the cold wasn't enough to drive the hope from his mind, his stomach chose that moment to make itself heard. The familiar and almost painful crunching and growling sound of his stomach met his ears and his companion's. She jerked her head around at the loud uncomfortable sound and he massaged his midsection. *It's been almost two days since I've eaten anything.* He knew that he could last a while longer. Hunger, like pain, could be ignored but eventually, he would have to eat something or risk passing out from hunger.

He leaned on the surrounding rocks for support to ease the stress of movement. He had to make it to wherever the wolf was taking him. He hadn't come all this way just to give up now.

The path began to straighten out and he could see it unfold in front of him. He had lost his sense of direction in the crags of the passage. He couldn't tell which direction they were going. He had a feeling that they were traveling a little more east than they were earlier, but he couldn't be sure of anything. He concentrated on putting one foot out in front of him, probing for rocks, putting weight on that foot then probing in front of him with the other. It was a tiring process.

They had been traveling for several hours when he noticed that he was moving faster. The wolf had been increasing her speed in the darkness as the night passed. He found that he had gotten used to the new way of moving his feet and he was walking much faster than he had been when they exited the tunnel.

The path they were on dipped down and he almost fell as the ground dropped away from him. The rocks surrounding the path were much smaller here and he had a clear view of the mountainside and the surrounding forest. He also had a clear view of the night sky. His waning mother was sinking to the west. *Have we really been traveling all night, already?* The passing of the night had completely eluded him while he was concentrating on his footing. Now he could relax a little bit. The shallow walls allowed more light onto his path, and he could see that where they walked now was much more worn by travel. The path tilted downward in front of him. The mountains surrounding them formed themselves into a bowl shape that made up a small valley, covered with dense trees. The path that the wolf was leading him on led straight into the deep protected woodland.

Seeing the valley was a relief. It was like coming home. The green of the trees themselves was a welcome change to the tans and stone of the boulders and rock that he had been traveling on. The forest looked like a soft green carpet, and he scrunched his toes against the hard cold rock in anticipation of having the feeling of warm dirt under them again instead of cold-as-death stone.

He glanced up into the waning night sky to thank his Lunar Mother for this paradise. The moon was setting in the western portion of the sky and as he was looking after her, the smile he was wearing slid from his face and was replaced with shock and disbelief. As he looked west, he saw a bright light in the sky. Much too low to be a star it was moving fast, and it was moving in their direction. He knew at once that it was the helicopter that had been pursuing them for the last few days. The wolf gripped the legs of his skins and pulled him down the path. The sudden movement tore his eyes away from the helicopter and he followed the wolf down the path.

The path was much smoother than what he had been walking on so far and he was able to jog. The path dipped down. He found himself more hopping down the path than walking. He turned his body sideways and skipped down the path using the broadside of his feet to brake with. The wolf was also hopping and bounding down the path. If he didn't know any better, he would have thought she was having fun.

The surrounding rocks gave way to trees. The trees were sparse, but no boulders intruded this far onto the steep valley wall. The path was now more dirt and pine needles than anything. He could now almost run with the black wolf that bounced off the dirt floor in front of him. The trail became steeper as they worked their way deeper into the valley. Instead of rocks and boulders, the path was now flanked by massive redwood trees. He almost stubbed his bare foot on a root that arched over the path in front of him.

Once they had made it down into the valley proper the soft dirt and pine-needle-covered floor of it met his feet and he felt more relaxed. He could move with a little more free-dom. No more scooting his feet out in front of him like some blind cripple, hobbling along on his way. Not that he had anything against cripples, but when one was running from federal or military agents hobbling was not the best way to keep ahead of said agents.

The wolf took off at a run and he followed close behind. The change in terrain left his hunger momentarily forgot-ten. The trees of the forest were tall but sparse so near to the valley wall. The dense woodland that he had seen from the boulder path was a ways off and they had to get there as soon as possible. Grass was able to grow in patches here and there away from the redwoods and the thick long blades massaged his feet. After scooting along with strict muscle discipline for so long he was grateful for the chance to open himself up and run. The wind was still very cool, but the working of his body got his blood moving and he was begin-ning to get warm again.

The sky was still black and strong with night's influence. The sun would not rise for another hour or so. By that time, they would have reached the trees. Before they entered the forest the wolf stopped running and sat down outside the natural boundary of the woods. He stopped as well and looked at her. *What is she doing now?* She sat there for a long time not moving, then, without warning or a backward glance, she entered into the forest, walking.

He walked after her and felt a strange warmth wash over him as he walked among the trees. He felt like he was being watched. The trees themselves had a very odd sense surrounding them and he made a point of staying very close to his guide and companion. He thought he understood why she had waited outside of this forest. There was something wrong here, something that made his skin crawl and she had probably been debating on whether she should even come into these woods. He was pretty sure that had he not seen the helicopter she might have led him around the woods. But with pursuit so dangerously close they needed shelter and the only shelter to be had was this strange forest. The unnatural warmth made him feel somewhat nauseous and it played havoc with his already unhappy stomach.

They walked through the woods. He found himself looking around himself more and more. His heightened sense of awareness was screaming at him to run away. His eyes were looking and darting all around him. He started seeing shadows dance and move from tree to tree. He would have sworn he saw eyes and faces leering at him. He knew he was being stupid but the sense of panic and fear that had gripped him in the tunnel earlier that night returned with a vengeance.

He looked down at the wolf by his side. She was walking with her back straight and head held proud and high. She must have been feeling the same thing he was, that they were being watched, but she kept her eyes and ears locked, pointed forward. Her ears didn't so much as twitch to either side of her as she walked in a straight line through the woods.

He was wide-eyed as the shadows seemed to be moving closer. He thought he saw them smiling at him. His stomach rumbled and he knew he heard a laugh barked out from somewhere. The wolf didn't respond to the sound.

He was miserable. He was jerking his head left and right as shadows flashed all around him. He couldn't focus on the blur of motion around them and his eyes were wide and wild looking. After some time, the fear of attack faded from his mind simply because he was exhausted. If these things were real and if they were going to attack, then let them come. Dying didn't seem so bad when compared with running forever from a tireless enemy that outnumbered you by thousands.

No, this is not where he would die. If a fight came, he would meet it with both hands, on his feet. The wolf kept walking in that same rigid fashion in the same rigid line she had been following since she entered these woods. He followed her example as she led him deeper into this strange place, this place where the shadows moved.

After some time had passed, he and his guide stepped into a small clearing in the trees. He was able to look through the forest canopy and see the stars. They were losing their brightness and soon there would be no stars left in the sky as they submitted to and disappeared in the new dawn.

The heat didn't seem so oppressive in this small space under the stars. He inhaled and realized that he couldn't smell anything. There was no scent at all. The trees, the dirt, even the wolf at his side, nothing smelled.

He looked down at his companion and she was sitting on her haunches looking straight forward as she had been doing since they had entered the clearing. He looked through the darkness at the trees. They were standing still, and everything was quiet. He was slightly disturbed at the thought of there being no smells here. And he was irritated that he hadn't noticed it earlier. Was the whole forest like this? The lack of scents was probably driving the wolf crazy. He knew that she hunted and was guided by her nose just as much as she was by her keen sight. This must be torture for her.

As he looked into the trees trying to penetrate the shadows, all at once there was movement all around them. He could see pine needles fall to the ground as trees were jostled by what appeared to be a tornado just outside the clearing. He could hear whooping and yelling, strange barks and laughter as shadows moved and whirled around them. They were standing in the eye of a storm of shadows and cruel laughter. The trees were being shaken and a cacophony of noise met his ears.

The wolf sat where she was, not moving, her eyes stayed locked in front of her. He turned his head trying to follow the shadows as they danced and twirled and blended into the wind. A wind that didn't touch the clearing itself but tore into the trees bordering the clearing.

Then just as quickly as the tornado started, it ended. They were standing in the clearing and the noise and movement around them stopped. The sudden stillness and silence made his ears howl and his skin crawl. There was something not right here. Six figures entered the clearing in the same instant.

He was looking ahead of him just as the wolf was. Two forms appeared in front of them while two more appeared at their sides. He felt the hairs rise on the back of his neck and he somehow knew that two more forms had appeared behind them. Standing in front of them was one human female and one very nasty-looking wolf. He was covered in a dark, uniform brown fur that covered his entire body. One of his ears had been scarred where something had taken off half of it. His eyes were gold like the she-wolf at his side but darker somehow. He could see no empathy or pity or fear in those eyes. He wasn't afraid but he felt a deep sadness for this wolf. Something terrible must have happened to him to make him so cold.

The girl standing next to him was covered in skins much like he was except she was wearing straight black bearskin pants. Her chest was left partially uncovered, while a strip of brown leather covered most of her breasts. Her skin was pale white, made even paler by the soft waning starlight.

"What are you looking at?" The girl spat at him. Her voice was rough and deep, almost like she hadn't spoken for a while. She shook her head, and her waist-long strawberry blond hair was loosened and fell over her chest covering her curves.

He moved his eyes upward and locked his blue-green eyes with her stark blue ones. She didn't pay him much attention but instead turned to his companion. "What are *you* doing here?"

His companion uttered a short burst of whines and barks. He found himself looking down at his companion, he hadn't heard her make this much noise ever.

The female looked at the wolf and then at him. She bent down and rubbed her hand along the neck of the big brown wolf at her side. They looked at each other for a while. The woman stood back up.

"You have us at a disadvantage." Her hard look softened and she smiled at his wolf companion. "You seem to know us, but we have no idea who you are." She stepped forward and offered her hand to him. "I'm Tasha."

He looked down at her hand. It was small and delicate looking. However, the man to his right was neither small nor delicate. If this woman spoke for this group, it would be unwise to underestimate her. He reached out his hand and she gripped it. Her hand possessed a startling strength, and he smiled as they matched strength in an iron grip of a handshake.

"I'm William."

She let go of his hand and turned to the wolf. She lowered herself and looked at her in much the same way as she had done with the brown wolf. He watched as the two females looked at each other.

After a time, Tasha stood up and shook her head. Smiling she turned back to William. "Your companion tells me you have been having some trouble with some agents."

William couldn't help his eyes grow wide as Tasha told him this. *My companion told you what? How?* Tasha must have picked up on his confusion because her laugh rang out through the clearing. It was full and beautiful. He hadn't spoken to another person in almost two years, and it was good to hear the sound of someone else's voice besides his own.

"Why, William, I do believe you seem shocked," she said with an overtly fake Southern belle accent. He wasn't quite sure if he should laugh or be insulted. There were a lot of weird things going on in these woods, the least of which was this strange girl who could communicate with wolves. *No stranger than you turning into a werewolf every full moon.* He ignored his own sarcastic retort.

"William, I'm joking with you." Her eyes hid a sense of mischief that he didn't trust. His eyes must have betrayed him because Tasha laughed out loud again. He remembered why he hadn't spoken to anyone for two years. He pulled his arms up and crossed them over his chest.

Tasha stopped laughing. "Wow, paranoid much? You really have no idea what's going on, do you?" Her expression changed from one of mirth to disbelief. She jerked her head down to the mostly black-furred wolf sitting next to him. His companion let out a series of barks and whines, different from her last outburst.

Tasha looked back at the brown wolf standing behind her. The wolf turned around and melted back into the forest. She looked down for a moment and she raised her eyes to meet William's. "I'm sorry. I didn't know. You really *don't* have any idea why you're here."

The sudden change in her attitude from one of mocking laughter to almost pity made his hackles rise. He took a deep breath through his nose as he tried to control himself. No, he didn't know what was going on, not really. He wanted some answers.

"Who are you?"

"I'm Tasha of the pack. I'm the alpha of those you see around you."

William looked around. The guy to his right was human while there was a female grey wolf off to his left on the other side of his companion. He looked over his shoulder to see two human females one was white with waist-long brown hair; the other was black with short black hair.

Tasha shook her head and breathed a deep sigh. "I know you must be confused. Unfortunately, I'm not the one to answer your questions." She looked down at the she-wolf. "You should have told him why he was here."

William looked back and forth between the two females, his guide and Tasha. He wasn't sure what he should do. He thought about just sitting down in protest until somebody told him something that made sense. He thought about waving goodbye and taking his chances with those federal agents who were hunting him for some reason.

As he stood there Tasha looked over at the guy standing next to him. She locked eyes with him and jerked her head toward the forest. The guy folded his arms in front of him. Tasha's look hardened and the guy unfolded his arms and disappeared back into the shadows of the forest. Tasha looked past him at the two girls who were standing behind him. She nodded once and the girls disappeared back where the guy had gone. He looked to his left and the wolf that had been standing there had also disappeared. The three that remained stood there in the clearing as the sky above them began to turn from black to dark blue as the morning approached.

Tasha looked between himself and his companion. Seeming to have made up her mind about something, she looked at William. "Look, I can't answer all your questions, but I can answer some of them. Come with me. It's not safe to talk here."

Tasha turned and he and his guide followed her back into the strange forest. As they passed through the trees, the sky brightened. The morning seemed to come a lot faster than usual. He couldn't see the sky through the dense forest canopy, but the world was getting brighter around them. He was able to make out the shapes of the trees and the underbrush. The greens and the browns of the woods came into sharper relief, and he didn't see any more moving shadows.

Tasha moved through the trees though she didn't run. Her strawberry-blond hair streamed out behind her as she ducked and moved under the low-hanging branches of her forest. She was attractive and willful. William stopped and shook his head. This whole thing was crazy, how could a woman call herself an alpha of a pack of only two wolves? *You're an alpha, aren't you?* Only when his Lunar Mother was full in the night sky and he sure as hell didn't introduce himself that way.

Tasha led them to a massive rock formation in the forest. It looked natural but somehow, he knew that it was man-made. The rocks rose above his head by at least two stories, about twenty or thirty feet. There was a moderately sized opening in the rocks that formed sort of a cave. It couldn't be very deep. Even with the brightening of the world around them as the sun rose his eyes couldn't penetrate the darkness of the cave.

Tasha sat down on a log that was not unlike the log he had prepared at his kitchen clearing back in his valley. He looked around this area of the forest. The trees were less dense than the areas they passed through to get here but they were not sparse. He looked around and saw evidence of human craftsmanship. He saw a rope tied to the trunk of a tree and disappear into the higher branches. He saw a sort of wall that had been built off to his right. There were gaps and crevices in the wall. If this were the eighteen hundreds that would have been a perfect barrier for Union or Confederate soldiers to hide behind and shoot at the enemy with almost no fear of being hit by enemy fire.

There was a large fire pit in the middle of the area. The dirt was brown and dry with use. Nearby in between several small trees that had grown very close together, there was a rope tied between them. The rope had been crisscrossed and wood lay on top of the rope to keep the wood that had been stacked there off the ground. Whoever these people that Tasha led were, they had done a lot of work, and by the look of things, they had been here a while.

Tasha motioned for him to sit down on a small round log on the other side of the fire pit. He sat down very cautiously. Tasha rolled her eyes at the apparent mistrust of her guest. "If I had wanted to hurt you in any way, I would have done it by now."

William could see the logic in it, but he wasn't about to lower his guard. Come what may he had chosen a long time ago, about the time he had moved into his valley, that he would meet his death fighting. He locked eyes with Tasha.

His companion was sitting an equal distance between both of them forming a triangle between the three of them.

He didn't see anyone else. He noticed that even here he couldn't smell anything. It was like he was in a hospital, not the middle of a forest.

Tasha studied him for a moment. She turned back to his companion. "What happened and how much does he know?" The wolf looked at Tasha and made a few soft barks and whines. After the wolf fell silent, Tasha nodded her head, took a deep breath, and shooting a vicious look at the she-wolf, she started talking. "Look, all this must seem extremely overwhelming right now. You must know that you're a werewolf, right?"

William feigned shock at the revelation. "No, I had no idea. I'm a... a... a WEREWOLF? Jesus, and here I thought everybody changed into a monster when the full moon was in the sky."

12

Tasha's eyes darkened and the smile that touched her lips did not reach her eyes. The she-wolf lay down and rested her head on her outstretched paws. William held his eyes wide in faux shock as he waited for her to tell him something he didn't know.

Tasha looked down at the ground. She jerked her head up and as she did so her long strawberry-blonde hair was whipped up and around and cascaded down her back. He couldn't help but glance down at the curves of her breasts. *Why don't you just go and grab them? I'm sure she'd love that.* He shook the thought away and he forced his eyes to meet hers.

The direction of his eyes was not lost on Tasha, and she smiled another mirthless smile.

"You're a comedian. It's nice to hear sarcasm every once in a while. I was just like you when I joined my first pack. I was twenty-two years old." She smiled at the thought. "I was so young, so naive. I thought I was some kind of demigod. I had power over my world, and I could make things happen for myself. I could have any guy I wanted, and I used that power foolishly." Her eyes focused on William once again. "I'm sure you've felt the pure rush of changing and all the things you can do, all those powers of superhuman speed and strength." He nodded. "You don't have to admit to anything. I already know. I can smell it on you. It's the smell of the forest and the kill. The smell of fresh, coppery hot blood that can never be washed away from your soul. I can see it in your eyes. And yet, your alpha tells me that you have lived out in some valley about a week's travel south of here."

"I have no idea what is going on, but I am the alpha of my pack." He thought it best to keep his responses brief for now. The one with the most information in a game like this had the upper hand and he was obviously at a huge disadvantage.

Tasha threw her head back and laughed, her rich full laughter filled the trees. "I knew you didn't know anything, but this is ridiculous." She looked at William and it was like he was looking into her eyes for the first time. Those deep blue orbs were beautiful. He found himself content being in this woman's presence. He hadn't felt this content or this happy ever. He loved her. Right then he would have done anything for her.

The she-wolf was on her feet, growling. She barked once and William could sense, even though he didn't care, that the hair along the she-wolf's back was raised. Tasha looked away from William and bowed her head to the she-wolf. Once she had looked away, William shook his head violently. *What the hell just happened?* It had really felt like he loved Tasha. He didn't love her; he had only just met her for Christ's sake.

"Forgive me, Aceso," Tasha said to the she-wolf. She

turned her head back to William while still speaking to the she-wolf. "He had to be shown this isn't a joke."

William averted his eyes and focused on a spot in the middle of Tasha's forehead. He wasn't going to have... whatever the hell had just happened, happen again.

Tasha cocked an eyebrow and smiled at him. "What's wrong, William? You can't look a woman in the eye?"

He hesitated for an instant. "How did you do that to me? What the hell just happened?"

"Pheromones."

"What?"

Tasha breathed a sigh and looked at William. "Pheromones are a natural scent that every creature has that directly affects the brain chemistry of others of their species. Like when a cat goes into heat. Her body produces a sort of natural perfume that the male cats can smell. That smell interacts with their brains, and they become horny and ready to mate with the female.

"You see, Will, since I was reborn during the crescent moon phase, I was gifted with the power of an extremely sensitive nose. I can smell things that even a wolf could not detect. More than that, I can change my biochemistry. I can produce scents and chemicals like a pheromone complex that works directly with the pleasure center of your brain, causing an intense feeling of pleasure and contentment, which mirrors love. In actuality, it was nothing more than your subconscious brain telling you to be extremely relaxed and horny."

She glanced over at the she-wolf standing next to William. The she-wolf was looking and watching Tasha's every muscle. The she-wolf's muscles were wound as tightly as steel springs. He had never felt her this tense. Were they in danger here? He shifted his attention back to Tasha.

"Your alpha was only able to detect what I was doing because I wanted her to. That, and the amount of pheromones I released." She arched an eyebrow. "You were able to smell something just now, right? Like a sweet perfume?"

He thought back to what had happened to him, and he had smelled something. He hadn't registered the smell at the time. It had smelled like his valley, running through the woods. It had smelled like blood and dirt, the thrill of the hunt and the pure joy of running with his pack.

"Yeah, I smelled something faint, like dirt and wind mixed together."

Tasha looked back and forth between the two of them. She looked at the she-wolf, who hadn't relaxed at all. "Should I formally introduce you to your beta, Aceso?"

He looked over at the black-furred she-wolf. She turned her head back toward him and he saw something in her eyes that he hadn't seen before. It was almost sadness, remorse?

"William, may I introduce you to the alpha of your pack, Aceso." Tasha motioned from him to the wolf. The wolf ducked her head while looking up at him.

William shook his head, "I told you that I am the alpha of my pack. This wolf is my guide. She led me here and she helped me escape numerous times but that doesn't mean she's my alpha, not by a long shot."

Tasha locked eyes with him. "You did say that you would follow her, didn't you?"

He started to protest but his mind reached back to those first couple of days on the open rock of the mountain. He had been angry at people, and he had thrown his money down on the ground in frustration. It was then that he had said that he would follow her. He looked at the she-wolf and back to Tasha. "I said I would follow her to wherever she was leading me but..."

Reading the shock and frustration on his face couldn't have been hard and Tasha looked sympathetic toward him. "Will, I understand your confusion." She shifted her attention to the wolf. "Aceso should not have accepted that as your oath of fealty."

Aceso, who only a few minutes ago had been nothing more to him than the black-furred she-wolf from his pack, his guide through the mountains, and his companion and comrade. She was his alpha? This was stupid. On the next full moon, he would either fight her and regain his status or just leave.

"Will, what good would leaving do?" Tasha asked as if she had heard his thoughts. "You still have to get to the mountain. Yes, Aceso should not have accepted your oath but right now you need her, and she needs you."

He looked down at the she-wolf and she met his eyes with hers. The look of remorse was gone, and it had been replaced with resolve. Aceso was once again the proud predator. She held his gaze as she sat down on her haunches, every bit the alpha of a pack. He couldn't help but burst out laughing. He couldn't help it. A week ago, he was the king of his valley. He was the alpha of his pack, and he was free to do as he wished. Now he was a fugitive from the government, he was subservient to a wolf, and he was talking to a woman who could control her biochemistry. This whole thing was ridiculous. But Tasha was right about one thing, what good would it do him to leave? He would be captured by those agents following them and then what? Spend the rest of his life in jail because he had decided to live outside of society? Even following a wolf was better than that.

He looked at the wolf. "Aceso, right? I'm William, though you probably already knew that." He leaned forward burying his face in his hands. Was he in some kind of dream? This wasn't so bad as far as nightmares went but going from the freedom to do anything and everything to being a beta in a pack of two, running away from their enemies, instead of fighting was just a bit of a shift. He needed some time to process all of this.

"Aceso brought you here for help though I have to wonder why."

"Who are you people? What the hell was that 'reborn on the crescent moon' stuff and how the hell do you know her?" he jammed a finger toward the wolf. "How do you know what her name is?"

Tasha looked at him through narrowed eyelids. "We are the pack of the brotherless. I first changed forms when the crescent moon was in the sky. I know Aceso's name because she told me, though she is not unknown to us."

"Well, that explains everything thank you, Tasha. I appreciate you clearing things up for me." He mopped his face with his hands and laughed into his palms.

"I know this is hard for you right now," Tasha said. "I told you I can answer some of your questions, not all." She stood up and looked down at him. "I can let you two rest here today. This place is safe, and no one will be able to track you inside this forest." She walked a little way into the woods. She turned around and their eyes met. "There's food in the cave if you're hungry. Those agents shouldn't be able to track you after you leave, either. My pack and I will lay down false trails of your scents so that if they are tracking you somehow, they won't know which way you traveled and you should have a clear path to the mountain."

She lowered her head. She looked as if she might say

something more but shook her head and disappeared into the forest.

They were alone again. He looked down at the she-wolf, Aceso. That was an odd name, but he didn't really care right then. He stood up, and as he did so, the sound of his stomach rumbling ripped through the woods and echoed off the rock formation and the surrounding trees. He rubbed at his midsection and made his way to the welcoming darkness of the cave.

The sky had brightened, and he was looking forward to the darkness of the cave. It seemed safe and he needed to sleep. His steps took him inside the cool black. He let his eyes adjust and he saw several boxes lining the walls of the spacious cavity. He was pleased to find an area of soft dirt covered with various furs. The bed looked inviting, and he immediately thought of his burrow. He missed his home. One day he would return there. But for now, he had to eat.

He opened a box that was along the wall and found it to be filled to the brim with berries. They had been dried and he grabbed a handful. They were sweet and filling. He thought maybe they had been raspberries but however these people had dried them, the process had shriveled the berries to something almost unrecognizable. There was something slightly off about the taste and he was unable to identify the things by how they tasted.

He closed the lid and opened another box. This one was much smaller and reminded him of his own little waterproof boxes he had owned. This box contained several dried fish and other strips of dried and salted beef. He took a piece of meat and ate the tough, chewy morsel. He ate a few more pieces of the meat. He knew that these had to be the winter stores for Tasha's group, and he didn't want to be greedy. He closed the lid on the box.

He lay down on the makeshift bed and pulled a deer skin up under his chin. He allowed his eyes to stay open and the blackness of the cave loomed over him. Slowly his eyesight adjusted to the almost pure darkness that surrounded him. The spreading daylight filtered in through the opening of the cave. The sunlight was muted, and he had no trouble ignoring the disturbance to the almost perfect dark. While he didn't feel peaceful at all, he did start to feel a connection between the darkness and himself. He could feel the darkness stare back at him. All creatures were capable of looking at the darkness, though few could withstand it when the darkness looked back at them.

The warmth of the skin and the sluggishness of his brain worked to pull him down to sleep faster than he would have believed. The last thought that he had before sleep overtook him was just how beautiful Tasha really was.

He was floating in the darkness. The floor of the man-made cave was gone, and he floated on nothing. He was calm here and he felt no fear, no anxiousness, and no pain. Floating here, he began to see a light. The light seemed to come from everywhere at once, soft as pure cotton. He wasn't sure he was seeing it at first. The infinitesimally small increase of the light around him confused him and he began to wonder if he was in fact seeing what he thought he was seeing.

The light continued to grow and with the light, warmth spread through his limbs. Here he had absolute freedom of movement. He rotated around himself as the light increased around him. He felt more alive here than he did even when he was running with his pack in werewolf form. No matter how bright the light grew it was somehow soft, lacking any harshness of the light that he had come to know from the sun or artificial sources.

There was a misty quality to what his eyes were seeing, and he came to rest, standing upright and he was able to walk. Gravity had him once more and he explored his new surroundings. He could make out his hands in front of him, though they seemed to shimmer or fade at the edges as if he were made of vapor instead of flesh.

He walked, aimless, in the soft white void. There was no detail here. There was only the light and him. Was this Heaven? He couldn't be sure. Was he sleeping again? He couldn't be sure of that either. He was just walking. He felt no fatigue and no hunger. He saw something. Just ahead of him, surrounded by swirls of air and mist was a form. It was a shadow among the swirling light.

The shadow stood upright, and it was tall. It stood a foot or so taller than him if he could be sure of the distances of this place. He wasn't sure of anything, not even his sight. Is this really happening? He took a step toward the shadow, and it moved away from him. The shadow was covered in the swirling light and remained obscure to him, showing no real detail. He took a few quick steps toward the shadow and, like a polar opposite magnet moves away from its twin, so too did the shadow stay a discreet distance away from him.

He was puzzled at the movement of the shadow and wondered where he was and if the shadow was in fact just a reflection of himself. He continued toward the shadow and the shadow moved away leading him through the white expanse.

He followed the shadow. His thoughts came slower to him, and he soon gave up trying to think at all. It was much more pleasant to just walk, following this shadow as he had been doing.

The shadow was his world. It was the only thing that mattered.

He had always been following it. He had always been here, walking without stress or tiring.

The shadow played with him, and he was happy to play the game he had always played. He took a step the shadow took a step away from him. He smiled as he shuffled forward and the shadow copied his movements, shuffling backward away from him.

This was fun, as fun as it always had been. His soul was light as it always had been, and he was just as happy as he always had been. The swirling light was always here, and the shadow was his ever-faithful companion.

He kept walking.

The white never changed, and the swirling never stopped. The shadow, his shadow, swayed as he swayed. His breathing was coming in shorter and shorter gasps, and he felt lightheaded. He always felt lightheaded, and he continued to sway as his shadow danced with him.

His stride was shorter than it had been a minute ago. His stride was the same short strides that he had walked with since the beginning of time. He heard a calming voice filter through his head.

'Relax, William.'

It sounded familiar. At once the voice called to his mind an odd form. It was a short thing that stood on four legs. It had two golden eyes. He didn't know why but he felt that he knew what this form was called even though he was sure that he had never seen such a creature before in his life. The color, however, was a strange mix of the white he had always known and the shadow that he always followed. The thing was somehow noble and strong looking though he didn't know exactly what that meant. It had a strange crown made of two things sticking up out of its head and its eyes were intense.

He smiled as his breathing continued to slow and shorten. The mist seemed to swirl around his eyes and his hands seemed blurrier than they were a moment ago.

'Relax.' The voice was as calming as it always had been. He had nothing to worry about here where he was, where he always had been.

His legs were wobbly, and he had trouble staying upright. He wanted to keep playing with his shadow. Why wouldn't his legs work right? He started to panic as his body seemed to be betraying him.

'William, it's time to go to sleep now.'

He felt his body stop walking and he wanted to do what the voice told him. He always felt so good when he did what the voice told him to do.

'Close your eyes, William.'

His eyes started to water, and he was so tired. Had he ever been tired before? He wasn't sure, but the question didn't help him to obey the voice. The voice was his world. He looked through his tears and all he could see was swirling white light. He wanted to sleep. He wanted to close his eyes. He tried to force his eyes to close but for some reason his body betrayed him.

'Lie down, William. Close your eyes. Sleep, now.'

He felt his legs buckle under the weight of his body. He crashed down to the ground and moaned as he discovered a new sensation that he had never felt before. It felt hot and uncomfortable. The white light had always felt soft and warm. This sensation was hot and stingy. The voice was still with him, and he was happy. The hot stingy sensation flew from his mind, and he happily closed his eyes, just as the voice told him to.

'Good boy, William.'

He liked being called a good boy. He felt so comfortable here.

'William?'

He smiled as he listened to the voice.

'William, you have done very well for me. Now you must sleep. You must sleep so you can be with me. You do want to be with me, don't you?'

He nodded his head as he rested on the white light. He wanted to be with the voice more than anything. It was what he had always wanted.

'Sleep now, William, sleep for me.'

He tried to relax as fully as possible. He had wanted this for as long as he had existed and now, he was going home. He was going to be with the voice forever. His heart leapt at the idea, and he was so excited his heart rate quickened.

'Relax sweet, William.'

His breathing slowed and he felt his eyes weigh down on themselves. He couldn't have opened them even if he had wanted to, and he didn't. All he wanted to do was sleep. He felt himself drift down deeper. He could see the white light that permeated through his relaxed and tightly shut eyelids. He was going to sleep, just like the voice wanted him to. That thought made him happy, comfortable, and even more relaxed.

He felt a sharp hot sensation rip through his body. His eyes flew open, and he was shocked to see a strange four-legged form standing next to him. He could see eyes just above where his body was melding with the form. He could make out white things underneath those eyes and he knew they were teeth.

As the hot, stingy sensation ripped through his body he realized that what he was feeling was called pain and that it was coming from this strange invader. The thing with teeth was biting him. He saw golden eyes and black fur and realized that he knew what those colors were. He remembered that this form was called a wolf. Why was it here? Where had the voice gone? The voice that had always been with him was strangely silent and he looked around trying to get up.

The wolf held him down and shook his body as he tried to stand up. He wondered what happened to his shadow. The shadow that he had always played with, surely it would help him get away from this vile creature that was hurting him. He shouted out for help but the only sounds that came out of his mouth were painful yelps.

The wolf continued to shake him and as the pain grew in intensity, he saw that they were not alone. The almost pure swirling light that had always surrounded him was now being stained by the appearance of several shapes. The forms coalesced from the light and came to resemble his shadow. He was surrounded by five or six of them. He looked down at his attacker smiling. He knew that his shadow and his friends would teach this thing a lesson for hurting him. As he looked down, he saw that the wolf was covered in black fur. He twisted around causing more pain as he felt an impulse to see something. He strained his neck to see that this wolf had a white starburst on its chest.

He stopped moving.

He recognized this wolf. Thoughts of a time before the white light and his shadow came to his mind, slowly, as if through a dense fog of dreamy forgetfulness. Soon his mind was flooded with images and memories.

He realized that this wolf was his guide and had saved him several times in the past few days. He remembered that the white light and his shadow had only existed for a short time. He hadn't always been here. He remembered his mother and father, his valley, and the moon. He remembered the stars and the old man, the sun. He stopped struggling and the pain in his side subsided.

It all came back to him in a rush.

The escape from his valley, the run through the crevice, the meal of rabbits. He and his wolf guide had shared everything.

He remembered the night escape from the helicopter and the hounds that hunted them.

As his memories slammed back into his head, he realized that the shadows were closing in on him and the she-wolf. He tried to stand up. His legs wouldn't move. He realized that his body was growing cold. There was no warmth in this place, only the bright, soft, white light and these shadows.

The shadows seemed to be grinning down at him. No matter how close the shadows moved to him, they never seemed to come into focus. They were always surrounded and obscured by the swirling white light of this place.

The she-wolf growled at the approaching shadows, but that did nothing to slow their approach. He was trying to make his legs obey his orders, but they remained where they were, useless on the ground. He tried to lift himself up on his elbows. He managed to get his back off the ground and hold his head up. It was like trying to roll a house-sized boulder up a hill. It was quite possibly the hardest thing he had ever done. He looked around him and the cold of this place increased, and he felt his body shivering, though he still could not make his legs move.

The she-wolf growled at the shadows as she moved around behind him and nuzzled his shoulder. He was grateful for the ease of the burden of his own body. He felt the wolf's warm breath upon his back. The sensation was almost as welcome as the ease of the pressure from his weakening arms.

The she-wolf came around him and stood by his side. As he struggled to remain upright on his elbows, he felt the warm spot on his back from the wolf's breath begin to grow. That was odd, this place should have robbed him of that warmth but not only did the warmth not dissipate, but it was spreading over his back and shoulders.

The pain in his shoulders and elbows eased and he found that he could lift himself up. As he moved and worked his muscles again the warmth seemed to spread through his body more rapidly, coating his cold useless limbs with comfort and strength. He looked up and saw the shadows continue to close in on them. Soon they would be surrounded, and he would know exactly what it was like to join with the voice that he had listened to so willingly only minutes before.

His legs twitched as his muscles remembered how to work. He willed his legs to move and soon his legs were folding up underneath him so he could stand. He looked at the shadows around him. They were very close.

The light that surrounded them seemed to dim but he still couldn't make out any clear detail in the shadows themselves. Where a normal person's head and eyes should be, he only saw a globulous mass of dark mist with no substance.

He tried to stand up, but his legs would not hold his weight and he crashed back down.

The shadows reached for him and the wolf with outstretched extensions of the shifting darkness they were made of. There were no fingers, but he knew he wanted nothing to do with these shadows, or this place, any longer.

He tried to stand up again, and again his legs gave out from underneath him.

The shadows reached out. He knew that he was going to die. Or something worse than that and he was going to meet whatever fate that awaited him at the hands of these things.

He forced his breathing to slow, and he concentrated on his legs. The muscles worked and blood pumped. He felt a wave of energy rush through his limbs, and he stood up. His legs buckled but he forced them to support his weight.

The shadows must have been shocked by this because their extensions hesitated for a moment, frozen, outstretched, reaching for him and his wolf companion. If these things were real, he would have been only an arm's reach away. True to the analogy, the shadow's extensions reached out for him, and he braced himself for what was to happen. He looked right at where the thing's eyes should have been and was not afraid.

An ear-splitting howl broke out through the mist.

The shadow stopped reaching for him and a massive shape flew in front of him. The shadow was eclipsed by this new shape and the shadow and substance of the thing melted and tumbled to the floor.

The surrounding shadows stopped reaching for him and they all turned their attention to this new presence. The shape was covered in black fur. It stood a good foot or two taller than he did. Crowning its head was two towering ears, sharp and majestic. Its massive arm and leg muscles bulged as it moved away from the downed shadow. The shadow faded into the white light and soon disappeared.

It turned around and its eyes flashed with hatred, and it howled. He wasn't afraid of this newcomer. He knew it to be a werewolf. Its body was covered in deep black fur, but its chest had a white starburst on it.

He looked around, startled to realize that his she-wolf companion was gone.

The shadows moved toward the werewolf. They spread out away from him as they moved to deal with this new threat. His legs had regained some mobility, and he took a step and then another to test his legs. He felt a blast from his side that lifted him off his feet.

The sudden pain and force of the blast knocked the wind out of him, and he struggled just to breathe. He was slung over the werewolf's shoulder before he knew what had happened and he was now facing back behind where the werewolf was running. He was being jostled and thrown around as the werewolf ran with him. Through the swirling white light, he could make out the remaining five shadows behind them. They were gliding through the light of this void. They didn't make any movements that he could see. They just moved over and through the white light like fish through water.

He could feel the speed at which the werewolf was running, her long strides eating up distance as she could only have been trying to get back to where he had started following the shadow. But no matter how fast the werewolf was capable of moving the shadows only moved faster and they were gaining on them.

The wound in his side from where the she-wolf had bit him was ripping with each bounce upon the werewolf's shoulder. He tried to reach back and cushion his side, but it was no use. His stomach was tight with the strain of protecting his gut and he had trouble breathing. He couldn't feel any wind not even at the speed with which they were moving. There was no wind here, no night, no sun, and no moon. Wherever he was he didn't want to stay here, and he wondered again at how he had gotten here in the first place.

The werewolf stopped running and used her inertia to throw him off her shoulder. She looked behind them and his eyes followed hers. The shadows were gliding toward them and would be upon them in seconds.

She grabbed him and hugged him to her in a full-bodied bear hug. He was engulfed by her warmth and her fur. He could smell the musty, earthy smell of her body and he was comforted by it. It was the only thing of the earth that he had smelled or experienced since coming to this place. He relaxed in the steel of the werewolf's embrace. His comfort was momentary as his ears were split by a high-pitched wail that would have broken glass.

The sound reverberated through the werewolf's body, and he felt the vibrations of it through her muscles and fur. He couldn't see anything but felt a great crushing force upon his body. He gasped for breath as he heard what he could only describe as wind rushing past him, the kind of wind you felt when riding in a convertible with the top down, only ten times stronger than that. He cried out into the maelstrom. That sound was going to make him go deaf. His weak and feeble human cry was instantly drowned by the howling that permeated his senses.

Just as quickly as it started, it stopped. He was still surrounded by fur and the smell of earth and sweat but the sound was gone leaving behind a different kind of howling in his ears. The werewolf let him go and he held his hands to his ears trying to dispel the thundering silence that engulfed him. He stumbled back away from the werewolf a few steps and looked at her.

She stood as she had in the void. He noticed that the opposite shoulder she had used to carry him was bleeding. He reached for her to comfort her wound, but she turned away from him and held up a restraining arm. She looked at him. He saw a deep pain in her eyes and his breath caught in his throat as he knew that the pain he felt was only a fraction of what she was enduring. She moved out of the cave. She stood in between the surrounding trees. Through the forest canopy a single ray of moonlight found its way down to the forest floor where she stood and let the moon light wash over her.

Moonlight?

Had he slept through the entire day?

He didn't have time to contemplate just how long he had been asleep. He had to help her. He looked around the darkness of the cave and threw open some more boxes. He could find nothing but food and various supplies. There were no medical herbs or moss or anything that might allow him to help her.

He stepped out of the cave toward her. He wanted to help her as she had helped him.

"I'm so sorry."

It sounded feeble to his ears, but she nodded to him. Her shining eyes softened and, through her immense pain, smiled at him. He felt better and as he studied the deep wound that slashed through her shoulder, he knew he had to do something, or she would bleed to death. But the werewolf didn't move from her spot in the moonlight.

He looked around the forest. There had to be something here that he could use to stem the bleeding. He ran around a little bit trying to find something, but the camp of Tasha's pack was almost sterile. His hands closed into fists in frustration. Why was this happening? He couldn't find anything, except dirt and wood, so he turned back toward Aceso, helpless.

When he looked at the creature in the moonlight he froze.

Standing there, bathed in moonlight, the werewolf was completely healed. There was no wound on her shoulder, and he had never felt more ridiculous. He had been looking for a way to help her when she didn't need any help. He shook his head and rested his hands on his knees. He was being stupid he knew, in werewolf form he had always healed fast too, but this was extraordinary. He studied her body and he saw no traces of her wound, no traces of anything except black and white fur, muscle, and claws. She looked down at him as he gaped, openmouthed at her miraculous recovery. She barked out a laugh.

He watched as she looked up into the night sky.

The moonlight cascaded down over her body. He watched as she bent her legs and threw herself into the forest. He ran out past the shaft of moonlight into the dense forest in chase, but she was already gone.

He stood there in the cool night air, alone in this strange odorless forest. He didn't even feel the ever-present sensation of eyes watching him. All forests have eyes, but he couldn't feel them now and he felt alone. There was no sound to break the silence that surrounded him.

He walked back toward the cave and stood in the single shaft of moonlight that had healed his protector. He looked up into the moonlight and let it bathe him for a long while. The moon light was comforting, and he didn't want to go back into the cave just yet.

He sat down on the cool dark earth in the pale white light. He was reminded of the dream he had just had, a dream that was very real it would seem. His wound and the wound of Aceso was more than enough proof of that. He thought back to how stupid he had been. He had let himself fall in love with a girl he had just met because of some biochemical scent that she had given off. He had entered some weird dream where the damage one sustains is very real. But more than that, he had given in to a strange voice without so much as a struggle and he had wanted to fight his alpha who was trying to protect him.

His alpha.

What was the world coming to?

Now he was readily admitting to himself, out here in the solitude of the night, in a sterile forest by himself, that he was in fact subservient to a wolf. A wolf that could change into a nightmarish beast that could rip him limb from limb anytime she wanted to it seemed.

He reached down to the forest floor and grabbed a handful of dirt. He washed his hands with the stuff and inhaled from his palms. He couldn't smell anything. Could Tasha and her pack really scrub all scent from the woods and earth? Rubbing the dirt from his hands he stood up and made his way back into the man-made cave.

He lay down on top of the skins of the bed not bothering to cover himself. He allowed his eyes to close. He wanted to sleep. He was exhausted beyond anything he had ever felt but sleep would not come. He lowered himself into a meditative state and let his body relax as much as he was able to, and he pulled into himself. He began to feel like his limbs were a mile long and he was a very small thing inside a huge alien body. Numbness settled over him. He had meditated like this many times. He had never achieved an out-of-body experience, but he was able to draw himself in toward the center of himself. His consciousness shrank and his physical body stretched out from him for what seemed like miles. He stayed in this meditative state till he felt sunlight come in through the cave entrance.

13

As the dawn approached and sunlight invaded the dark of the cave, he opened his eyes. He had put off the inevitable for long enough. He stood up and stretched. He was tired. More tired than he cared to admit, his body and mind were responding like he had been coated in tar. He wiped at his eyes and stretched. His alpha should be back soon and then they would have to leave this place, this forest that was protected by Tasha and her 'pack of the brotherless,' whatever that meant.

He stepped over to the boxes and grabbed a handful of dried berries and some dried beef. He didn't know when he was likely to eat again. He felt guilty eating the foodstuffs of other people, but Tasha had said to help himself if he was hungry.

With his stomach satisfied, he exited the cave. He was almost surprised to see Aceso, once again just a black and white she-wolf, lying down right outside the cave. She lifted her head as he seated himself on the dirt next to her. She didn't make a sound, she looked at him. He looked at her and met her eyes.

"I never got a chance to thank you last night."

Aceso cocked her head to one side. She looked puzzled and he began to wonder if in fact what had happened had been nothing more than a dream within a dream.

"You, ah, you saved me from those things in that dream. You, you got hurt."

Aceso nuzzled his arm and nodded her head once. He looked into her eyes, and he knew that she knew what he was talking about. It had been no dream. She stood up and walked out past the fire pit. He watched her as her tail swung as she made her way over to the spot where she had stood last night in the shaft of moonlight. She turned around and met his eyes. She lowered her head in a bow.

Her hind legs expanded rapidly, growing in width but lengthening as well. Aceso's fore legs contorted as they shot out from her body, growing in length and expanding in muscle. She hunched over as her tail lengthened; her neck shortened as her snout shrank in on itself pressing into her face. Her ears reached up, growing tall and pointed on top of her head.

William watched her change, each contortion of her body he knew well, but when he changed it brought about a searing agony, while Aceso's face was serene as she changed. Aceso stood up on her hind legs hunching forward as her whole body seemed to melt and dissolve in front of him into a shapeless formless mass, a shadow. William's eyes went wide in terror and recognition. Then the shadow was gone.

Standing in front of him, where Aceso had been, now stood a seven-foot-tall werewolf. She was covered in black fur except for her chest, which carried a white starburst. William stared in shock. *What the hell was that? Did I really see that... that thing?* Shaking the thought away as something he must have imagined, he stood up and met the creature's eyes.

"William, I am Aceso. I have a grave apology to make to you." She looked to the sky for a moment before continuing. "I'm sorry I accepted your oath of fealty. I know that was wrong. I did it so I could better protect you and escort you to the Mountain."

He held up his hands. "What are you talking about, 'the Mountain'? Tasha mentioned that, too. What are you saying and where are we going?"

"We're going to the mountain to the north. I believe you call it Mount Shasta. Once we get there, you'll be put to the challenges of the Tower. You will be tested, William. You may die."

William looked at her with wide eyes, "Wait a minute, 'die,' like dead dead, pushing up daisies, dead?"

Aceso nodded, "Yes, William. You are one of us, a Shape shifter, or at least, you have the potential to be. The Tower will test your will, and abilities. The City under the Mountain is our home, it is kept secret and you will be pushed to your limits, or you will die. It is done for the protection of our kind and our home. Those Shadows aren't the only things that'll be hunting you now."

William listened to what Aceso was saying, but none of it made much sense, he shook his head and lowered his eyes to stare at the ground. "Does this have something to do with those... those things? What if I refuse? Who the hell do you think you are."

Aceso nodded, "We are all that's left of the Shape shifters of the world. Two thousand years ago we numbered in the thousands, and there were more races of shifters, as well. The Bultungin in Africa, the Berserkers and bear clans of the frozen north of Europe, and even, some say, weretigers, or the equivalent, in southern Asia and India regions. Now, the only known race of shifters are were-wolves, and we number worldwide in the hundreds, only."

"As for what you encountered last night in the Whyte Plain, those things are the Shadows of the Whyte Plain. They stalk us somewhere between waking and dreams. They feed on us and corrupt everything they touch." Aceso paused for a moment looking at the bewildered human, "William, I'm sorry I didn't tell you these things earlier. I travel with you in my original wolf form because in that form I can better avoid the darker things in this world. The trap you fell into last night was set by the Shadows. They are our deadliest enemies and prevent us from moving the way we used to. Right now, you're nothing but a werewolf, controlled and influenced by the Lunar Mother. Maybe it was that raw untapped power the Shadow's felt and were drawn to."

"The Shadows, those things that tried to..." he couldn't finish his sentence. It wasn't just the Shadows that caused him to end up in that dream last night. He had wanted to go, and had gone willingly. He wasn't ready to face that reality just yet.

"Yes," Aceso spoke before William felt he had to continue. "They are continuously trying to influence the world with their corruption and evil. We fight and kill them whenever we can, but they are far more dangerous than any threat you could imagine, and many, many Shape shifters have fallen to them, adding to their numbers."

William let the words settle down around him like a fog. How easily would it have been for him to have been taken by those things only a few weeks ago.

"Wait, but that was only a dream, right? It wasn't really real, was it?"

Aceso shook her head, "William, it was as real as I am and the dirt underneath you. The Whyte Plain is like a pocket dimension that we Shape shifters have used for thousands of years for travel, recruitment, study, communication, protection, it was everything we needed. Through it we were able to accomplish so much. Only now it is as you saw last night, a barren, mist shrouded place, where the Shadows hunt us relentlessly. The Shadows attack us whenever they can. You didn't know what was happening, and thus were an all too easy target for them to draw into the Plain. They are attracted by large groups of us. In this forest there are eight of us. Our combined energies would have drawn them here to capture and kill as many of us as possible."

He looked at her. "What were those things, Aceso? What did they do to me? Were they using more pheromones? How did you find me in that place?"

Aceso lowered her eyes and shook her head. "William, I'm your alpha by your oath. Because of that, I was able to feel where you were and was able to track you down. You can do the same thing with me; the bond works both ways. If it wasn't for that, I never would have found you and you would be lost to the Whyte Plain roaming it as just another mindless Shadow. They have the ability to affect our minds and our desires on a level that goes beyond even what Tasha or even Elder Ansuya, as one of the most gifted Trackers of the Mountain, can do. We aren't sure why they can affect us so deeply, but it is because of that that they are so dangerous. As to what they are, you're a smart, young man, I'll leave that to you to figure out." Aceso visibly shivered as she said this part.

"Aceso, why am I here? What did I do to deserve this?" William asked quietly.

"What alerted us to your existence was the information from some of our allies that the local and state governments were looking for you. You don't have a record, so the amount of money and resources that was being spent to find one random missing young man in central California led us to believe that you were more than just a random missing person."

"The vampires of the world have deeply running influences and they have found a way to hunt us before we are reborn. Before we can find new Shape shifters and bring them to safety in the Mountain. This is why finding you and bringing you to the Mountain is so important. We need every Shape shifter, to help fight, not only the vampires, but the Shadows, and cleanse the Whyte Plain so we can start fighting the vampires from a position of strength, instead of hiding in our mountain getting weaker by the month."

"Why does a vampire want to kill me? I'm a nobody."

"They want to kill you, because you are a Shape shifter. We are the only things standing between the parasites and the complete subjugation and genocide of the human race." Aceso replied flatly.

He sat there for long moments. Trying to process everything that she was telling him. He could bring himself to understand a few basic concepts. Vampires were real, apparently, and he was being hunted by them because of what he was. He almost died and the only reason he was still alive was because Aceso accepted his oath, whatever the hell that meant. And he was going to Mount Shasta to possibly die anyway if he failed a series of tests. Tests that he had no idea what they might be. He looked around the quiet, sterile smelling woods around him with a wistful glance, and it reminded him of just how much he wanted to be back in his valley, before any of this had happened.

"I should not have brought you here." Aceso said quietly, "The pack of the brotherless is not spoken of. I will protect you and shield you from now till we get to the Mountain. If it really was vampires that sent those agents after you, they won't be so easily dissuaded by Tracker tricks. But maybe Tasha will keep her word, and it will buy us some time at least. I have been ordered to bring you to the Mountain and I will. You are very precious to me, as you are to all our people."

He looked up at her. Aceso shrank and reformed back into her original wolf form. He threw his hands up into the air in frustration. Aceso stood there on all fours once again, nothing more than a beautiful she-wolf. He stood up and walked over to her.

As he approached her, she turned around and started jogging into the forest. His brain was numb with everything that had happened, and his fatigue didn't help his state of mind at all. Tasha and her pack were nowhere to be seen. He made his legs move, one in front of the other. He leaned forward and his legs jerkily threw themselves out, one in front of the other. He soon found his rhythm and he followed Aceso through the forest. Aceso was dodging in between the trees at a speed that was incredible considering the injury she had just recovered from. He couldn't help but wonder why she had run off into the forest last night. Did she run off to hunt? He didn't know and he probably wouldn't get an answer from her even if he asked. In the course of two days, he had slept an entire day and found out more than he ever wanted to know, but not enough to make sense of anything.

At least he knew where they were going, Mount Shasta.

That must have been the mountain he had seen off in the distance with its snowcapped top. That thought made him feel a lot better. Maybe this trip wasn't going to be as long as he thought. After what Aceso had just told him though, he was wishing that the journey would take as long as possible.

14

Through rain, forest, cold sunshine, and the grassy flat land leading up the mountain slope, they ran. William doggedly followed Aceso as she ran with more and more speed. It was as if she was being driven by some unknown force or pull towards the mountain.

The time passed and the miles flew under their feet. Even though they could see the mountain it still took over two days for the two of them to cross the distance from Tasha's forest, and make their way half way up the mountain slope. They stopped only under the cover of the mountain's various stone outcroppings. It was the only relief that William got from the freezing rain that had been driving itself through his clothes and chilling him to the bone.

Eventually they came to a large rock outcropping that formed a deep depression in the side of the mountain. It was more a small cave, with the back of the cave shrouded in deep shadows. Aceso didn't stop but walked underneath the rock overhang into the natural shade of the cave. He noticed that her head was low, and he knew that something was bothering her. She seemed apprehensive and he wondered why. He could almost feel a sense of fear coming from her and he wanted to reach out to her, to pet and scratch her head, to let her know that everything was going to be all right. Of course, he had no idea if everything was going to be all right. He was lost in this world that he found himself in. Who was he to tell this proud wolf that everything was going to be all right?

Aceso walked to the very back of the small cave. He walked after her letting the shadows protect him from the sunlight. Aceso was studying the dark, back wall of the cave. He wondered what it was she was looking for. Aceso broke the silence by letting out an ear-splitting howl that shook the walls around them. He recoiled from the sudden noise that washed over him. He put his hands to his ears as he tried to recover his hearing. None of his pack had ever made a sound this terrible. He pressed his hands closed around his ears, as he tried to insulate himself from the thunderous noise that echoed and reverberated off the small cave's walls.

Aceso let the sound die and she studied the wall once more. He let his hands loosen from around his ears. The ringing in them would stop, eventually. At least he hoped so. He wouldn't be able to hear anything with his ears ringing the way they were now. He shook his head trying to clear the sound out of his head. As he was doing that, however, a new sound met his ears. This one was of a soft grating sound, almost the sound of fingernails on a chalkboard. But this sound was deeper, more mineral. As he tried to figure out if this sound was just his ears or something else, his eyes widened as he noticed the back wall of the depression that had been shrouded in dark shadows was moving.

Aceso sat where she was and watched as the wall opened into a gaping blackness where solid rock had once been. He shook his head and stared at the moving wall. *It's like some secret passage straight out of Scooby Doo.*

The rock wall stopped moving and Aceso entered into the perfect black void disappearing from his vision. He was left standing there wondering what he should do. He had followed Aceso without question for days and through miles of terrain. *It's a little late to be getting cold feet now, don't you think?* He looked down at the ground and with a last glance at the gentle sunlight of the morning he followed where Aceso had gone and disappeared into the darkness.

There was no light.

He began to grope around in the perfect darkness. He wanted to turn around and look at the sunlight. As he did so, the scraping sound met his ears. The opening of the cave that Aceso and he had just come from was closing. There was a part of him that panicked at seeing the sunlight eclipsed by the black void. It was all he could do not to break out in a run and dive back outside. He began to hyperventilate, and he broke out in a sweat. This perfect dark and unknown void scared him. At that moment he wanted nothing more than to be out in the glorious sunlight. *It's now or never.* Just when he was about to make a break for the ever-shrinking exit, he felt a soft, warm, and familiar presence at his side.

He reached down and felt Aceso's ears and head. He felt calmness return to his body, and he slowed down his breathing. The shrinking sliver of sunlight disappeared entirely. He was with Aceso, but they were shrouded in perfect darkness.

He couldn't see anything. All he knew was that he was afraid of this place for some reason and no amount of rational thought could assuage that feeling of panic. The only thing that kept him standing in place with dignity and not running toward the exit and madly scraping at the rock with his fingernails was the calming presence of Aceso.

The perfect void was shattered by a flash that was as bright as magnesium. His eyes were open, but he wished they hadn't been. He was blinded by the sudden light. He closed his eyes, trying to erase the blue-violet retinal burn from his eyes. He wouldn't have been able to see anything at the moment anyway. He blinked his eyes hard and long, trying to aid in their healing process. While his eyes were closed shut, he felt Aceso leave his side. He ripped his eyes open and through the fading blue-black haze that covered his eyes, he saw Aceso walking away from him.

She was flanked on either side by giant humanoid forms. The one on the right of Aceso was grey with black and brown streaks that ran down the whole of its back. Its tail was standing up behind it proudly as it walked with an easy gate. His claws were drawn in at his sides. The one to the left of his alpha was mostly brown with some reddish-brown streaks along his arms and legs. His ears were tall and far longer than the wolf to the other side of Aceso, his tail was held high as well. The two werewolves escorted Aceso away from him deeper into the caves. He scrambled forward to move toward her but was stopped by an iron grip on his clothes.

"ACESO! Where are you taking her?"

He struggled against the grip on his vest. He watched in panic as Aceso walked off down a tunnel that made its way deeper into the mountain. She didn't turn around. She did glance over her shoulder back at him. Her eyes held a look of perfect sympathy and sadness.

He struggled trying to get to her. Aceso barked back to him then she turned her head around and continued walking away from him. He didn't take his eyes off her, and he fought harder and with greater desperation. His only thought was to be at Aceso's side. If she needed help, he had to be there. He owed it to her to help her.

He managed to slide out of his vest and the grip that held him in place. He sprinted after Aceso down the tunnel that she had disappeared down. He took a few steps and was gathering speed when he slammed, face first into an immovable object that appeared out of nowhere.

His world exploded in pain and light. He stumbled back from whatever he had just run into as he tried to relearn how to breathe. He almost fell down but by some miracle he was able to keep his feet and looked around as his lungs took in small gasps of air, keeping him conscious. He gripped at the pain in his abdomen and chest as he looked around. He looked to his right and towering over him was a massive beast with huge, pointed triangle ears that crowned his head. His face and body were covered in brown fur. His eyes were pure molten gold and shined with an inner light that looked through him in absolute apathy. William could see no forgiveness or empathy in those eyes, and it was all he could do to stand his ground.

The pain in his torso was fading and his eyes could see clearly, for the most part. The brown werewolf that stood over him made no movement to attack or restrain him. His tail was hanging behind him. It was not limp, but not upright in an attack position either. William stood there allowing his body to take deeper and deeper breaths until he was breathing normally again. He looked around the tunnel where they stood. He noticed that the light that illuminated their surroundings was emanating from a single torch that was held to the tunnel wall in a cast iron bracket. It was medieval in design, and he wondered if that torch would lead him to some form of medieval torture.

Looking behind him, William saw the entrance that he and Aceso had come through looked like a solid rock wall. There was no seam and no sign that there had ever been anything other than solid rock there. From the wall, a wide tunnel stretched out and down into the mountain. The walls were smooth and black. The ground he was standing on was smooth and black as well like it was covered in the purest black marble or obsidian.

He turned away from the exit that wasn't there anymore. He raised himself up to his full height and faced the massive werewolf that stood over him. "Where are they taking Aceso?"

The werewolf stood.

"Who are you?"

The werewolf folded his arms across his chest still not answering.

"Well, you just stand there like an idiot while I go find out what happened to my friend."

William tried to get around the massive wall of flesh and muscle that blocked his path. The werewolf moved to stay in front of William. He dodged to the right and then cut back to the left. Every time, the werewolf was a half-step ahead of him and stayed in front of William, not yielding an inch.

"You son of a bitch, move or talk to me, What the hell is this place and where is Aceso being taken?" The werewolf didn't respond in any way. William was going to make a break for it. He allowed his muscles to tense as he prepared to throw himself down the tunnel away from the silent sentry.

"I wouldn't try that if I were you."

William stopped cold as the human voice spoke out against the cold stone of the tunnel. He turned around and saw a rather large man coming out of a tunnel that William hadn't even noticed. He was wearing regular clothes. He had on blue jeans and a button-up shirt that was a vibrant orange. His skin was black as a starless night and the white of his eyes jumped out of his dark face. He even wore a pair of black and deep blue shoes. The man could be called attractive, and he was powerfully built with broad shoulders and huge hands that swung easily at his side as he walked.

William watched as the newcomer approached. "Try what?"

The man laughed deeply and pointed back at the werewolf that was standing behind William. "You try to run off down that tunnel again and Ares might take your head off."

William looked back at the large werewolf. He took one last look down the tunnel where Aceso had disappeared. "Where did they take Aceso?"

The newcomer raised an eyebrow. "Where they took her is none of your business."

The man closed the distance to stand within inches of William. William held his ground. The two men stood about equal height. The guy was about twice as wide as William was, but he was betting on his speed and agility to equal things out if it came to trading blows with this man.

"The only skin you should be worrying about right now is your own, pup." He started to walk around William and William rotated to continue to face him. "This is The Mountain. This is my home and while you are in my home you will follow my instructions, or you will be punished... severely if need be." The man stopped and looked William in the eye.

William met that cold stare. "Who are you?"

He didn't seem to move. Yet William's stomach exploded with pain and once again he couldn't breathe. His legs buckled under him, and he fell to his knees. He gasped for air as he tried to stand up. The man towered over him. His huge hands had tightened into massive fists.

"Rule number one, pup, you don't talk unless I tell you to."

William struggled but was able to regain his feet with more effort than he wanted to admit. He noticed that the werewolf had a look on his face that remained completely passive. It took his eyes off William and looked at the broad-shouldered assailant who was now standing in front of William. William allowed his eyes to drift from the werewolf back to his attacker.

The guy was talking again. "You have pretty good stamina, pup. Usually, new blood has the good sense to stay down once I drop them." William tensed his abdomen and readied himself for another attack. But the blow never came. Instead, he turned his back on William and walked a few steps away down the tunnel he had emerged from.

William stared after the man as he disappeared down the dark shaft. He felt a rough shove from behind. He stumbled forward and looked over his shoulder. He saw the werewolf motion down the tunnel in front of him. *Push me like that again, and you and I are going to have some serious problems.* He knew that he couldn't take the werewolf as he was now. But every month brought a new full moon, and then he would see about who was doing the shoving. As William entered the tunnel the werewolf grabbed the torch from the bracket and followed him down the dark passage.

His new guide was walking down the tunnel. He was almost strolling. He didn't seem to care that William had joined him. They walked in silence. William was walking in between the two just as Aceso had done. The flames from the torch danced and moved their shadows along the wall. William could smell the werewolf. He didn't smell unlike

Aceso, he put off the same kind of earthy musky smell that she did. There was something different about his smell though. His smell seemed bloodier somehow. There was power and strength in his smell. There was no scent coming from the guy though, neither a sweaty unclean smell nor a garish scent of deodorant or body spray. William couldn't smell him at all, that may have been the point.

The silence stretched out between them. The tunnel wound its way deeper into the mountain. William wanted answers and he was going to get them.

"Who are you?"

He was slammed up against the smooth tunnel wall before he knew what happened. A large human forearm was pressed up against William's throat and he found it rather difficult to breathe as he was forced to look into the dark brown eyes of his guide. He grabbed the man's arm and was now pressing against the iron grip trying to lessen the pressure against his windpipe. His eyesight began to blur, and he was able to suck in less and less air. Tears began to drip from his eyes as the life was being crushed out of him. The strength was draining from his body as he was held in place against the wall.

William had always considered himself to be an honorable fighter. He never took low blows and was always ready to fight according to the rules of boxing and other forms of martial arts. His vision was darkening around his eyes, and he knew that he might die here. In his desperation, he slammed his right knee up in between his attacker's legs.

The man grunted and pulled away from William. Air rushed back into his lungs, and he reached out and gripped the guy's neck. They were locked in twin death grips. The other man's large hands engulfed William's entire throat. William's hands couldn't quite wrap around the guy's neck to apply squeezing pressure. That was ok. William let his thumb find and press into the man's Adam's apple, the ultimate weak spot. The guy immediately let go of William's neck and punched through William's arms, breaking contact. William gasped and put his hands to his throat. He coughed as he massaged his neck. He backed away from his assailant and pressed his back against the cool stone of the tunnel wall. The other guy breathed heavily for a few moments and looked over at the werewolf, who hadn't moved. He raised himself up, recovering from William's attack easily. "In the future, you'll call me Mr. Davis. You got that, pup?"

William stood up straight. He looked the man in the eyes. William saw pain and hatred there. He inhaled through his nose, controlling his own anger. "OK, Mr. Davis. Who are you guys and where did they take Aceso?"

Mr. Davis didn't answer. Instead, he turned away and started walking back down the tunnel. William had half a mind to stay where he was and refuse to go any further till he got some answers.

Even as he thought that though he knew that it would be a fruitless gesture. These guys held all the cards, and they knew it. The only way for him to find out where they had taken Aceso was to play along. Tasha had spoken of 'The Mountain.' He was here and whatever he was supposed to learn was here. It wouldn't do either him or Aceso any good if he just quit now. He wasn't sure he could ever come back if he left anyway. There were answers for him here. He just had to be patient. He caught up with the two of them and continued to walk down the dark tunnel, the torch dancing with their silent footsteps.

Mr. Davis glanced over at the werewolf and back to William. He had a bemused look on his face as if there was some huge joke that William was not in on. William kept his face even and didn't show his displeasure at not being aware of what was so funny.

"I usually have to carry most of the new pups in from this tunnel," Mr. Davis said to no one in particular.

William looked over at Mr. Davis and saw that he was smiling at William's confusion. "What do you mean?"

"I mean, that most of the pups that come in through that door piss me off like you just did. The only thing is they don't know the first thing about fighting and they usually pass out. It was a test, my test. I'm not saying you passed, not by a long shot. But you did manage to get me off you. Regardless of how you did it. The fact is you did it."

They walked a short distance before Mr. Davis stopped and turned to William. There was a hard look in his eyes. "Now you listen to me, pup, and you listen good. For the next several hours, your ass is mine. You got that. I could kill you and nobody would question it or even care. I was placed in charge of all the new pups that come in here. You either get with my program or I'll kick you out of here faster than you can blink."

Mr. Davis turned from William and headed off down the tunnel again at a brisk pace, much faster than before.

William walked in silence taking in what Mr. Davis had said.

William saw a faint blur of light that must be the end of the tunnel. He had lost track of how long they had traveled or how far they had walked but it seemed that at least this part of the journey was ending. They walked the remaining distance down to the end of the tunnel. Ares placed the torch that he was carrying into a cast iron bracket that hung inside the cave wall and doused the bright orange flame.

Leaving them, momentarily at least, to content themselves with the dimness of the tunnel.

The tunnel mouth opened up into a cavernous space. The area stretched out in front of them as far as he could see. The cavern housed a massive collection of structures that looked to be glossy black children's building blocks. Everywhere he looked was some kind of building. The whole cavern, from one wall to the next, was filled with stacks upon stacks of black square buildings. The only thing he could describe it as was a city. But the city was a jumbled mess. The stacks of buildings never rose more than five high. From his vantage point above the sprawl of the buildings, he would have expected it to have roads. There weren't any that he could see only slight gaps in between the buildings. He felt like he was looking down on a massive labyrinth, a labyrinth that didn't have a clear way to navigate through it.

The city disappeared back into the haze of sightlessness as the massive underground cavern stretched unimaginable miles off into the distance. Off to the sides of the cavern, the buildings pressed right up against the cavern walls. To his right, however, he saw something that should not have existed. Nestled against the wall of the cavern and hugged by black buildings were hundreds of acres of forest. The evergreens rose to scrape the very ceiling of the cavern. There was no wind here, so he couldn't smell the forest, but the green foliage that he did see told him that he was not imagining it. As impossible as it was, he was looking at a full underground forest. The sight made him feel easier and less tense almost immediately. There was a matching forest off to the left and he could swear that he could see another patch of green further in the distance.

There was light here but it didn't come from the sun. It

appeared that the cavern ceiling itself was illuminated by a soft white light, though he couldn't identify the source. As he stood there trying to take in everything he was seeing, he thought back to his forest, the old grey, Aceso, and all the events that had happened, and sacrifices over the years that had all led him to this moment. The journey had been anything but easy, but Aceso had done what she had told him she would. His journey was finally over. William stood in shock and awe at the pure scale of this place.

Mr. Davis spoke, breaking through his thoughts. "Welcome to The City Under the Mountain, pup."

EPILOGUE

Kenneth once again found himself inside Mark's office. It had been some time, over a week, since Kenneth had received any update on the whereabouts of William Setford and it was past time that he got those answers. Mark was sitting behind his desk hunched over some reports. His hair was disheveled and he looked strained. The man had probably got very little sleep in the past few days.

"Mark. What have you been doing?"

The statement hung in the air and Mark could do nothing but look at him. Finally, the man shook his head and heaved a sigh. "I've been working, that's what I've been doing." He ran a hand through his disheveled hair. "I have been tracking down every lead I can for some maniac on the east side of Compton. He's killed five people already. I've been working on a drug bust to close down a ring of gangs that have been pushing drugs to the high and middle schools in the area. I have my boss breathing down my neck about some store fronts that are out of code and haven't replaced some equipment to be in compliance."

He stopped and looked up at Kenneth, "But other than that; I've been twiddling my thumbs! What can I do for you, Mr. Pacifico?"

Kenneth smiled at the young man. Yes, Mark had gotten very little sleep in the past week. Beyond human perception, Kenneth moved around the desk and had Mark's throat in his hand and pinned him up against the wall. The shock on the man's face was very satisfying.

"Mark, I do not make requests. When I say that I need something done, you do it. There is nothing else for you to do. I want that man found. Do I make myself clear?"

Marks eyes were bulging from lack of oxygen. The man frantically nodded his head as far as Kenneth's hand would allow. Kenneth dropped him to the floor.

The man gasped for a moment on his knees. He massaged his neck and kept his head down for a moment. He coughed hard and looked up. He got back on his feet still massaging his neck. "That was uncalled for."

Kenneth frowned. "I decide what is called for and what is not. Remember your place, and maybe I won't have to remind you of that in the future." Kenneth knew that he was channeling his own master. Mark was just a human, and humans deserved to be treated like this. He wouldn't mind seeing them all in collars and chains like it had been before.

Mark dropped his eyes and turned around to a pull-out board from the wall and therein was an enlarged map of Northern California. There were circles and lines all over it. Even Kenneth couldn't tell what it all meant.

"Here was the last known place of the man you've had me tracking," Mark said pointing to a place on the map. There was a large purple circle around the point, about thirty five miles in diameter according to the key scale. "This is the radius our search teams have been out to so far." He pointed at the purple circle. "There has been no trace of them beyond our last known point." Mark shook his head and indicated to other places on the map. "We have tried backtracking and searching over countless miles of rocky, mountainous terrain hoping to find something. I've pulled in helicopters, blood hounds, park rangers, you name it; I've tried it. The man you are looking for has simply disappeared."

He looked up and saw how that did not please Kenneth. "No one simply disappears, Mark. I want him found."

The cop rested his hands on his desk. "The guy is a ghost right now. There is no hope of us finding him. The only thing we can do now is wait for him to pop up on the radar somewhere else. I know this guy can live in the woods for years on end. He survived at least one winter out there; he could do it again. But I simply don't have the men or resources to keep sinking man hours into a hunt that has led, and will probably continue to lead, to nothing."

Kenneth knew the man spoke truthfully, but that didn't mean he liked hearing it. He really wanted to break something. But he restrained himself and continued to look at the blown-up map of Northern California. It all looked so flat and bereft of civilization, with only small pockets of life they called towns separated by hundreds of miles, with the bottom half of that ridiculous volcano dominating the northern most border of it all. *So, William, it looks like you've won this round. But I always play the long game, and this game is far from over.*

ABOUT THE AUTHOR

Christopher Scherrer is an emerging author of dark urban fantasy. He is a veteran of the United States Navy and Army where he served in both the enlisted and officer ranks. He is married and both he and his wife live with their daughter in Florida.